SHE DANCED WITH A REDFISH

SHE DANCED WITH A REDFISH

CAROLYN NUR WISTRAND

University of Louisiana at Lafayette Press
2025

© 2025 by Carolyn Nur Wistrand
ISBN 13 (paper): 978-1-959569-18-3

http://ulpress.org
University of Louisiana at Lafayette Press
P.O. Box 43558
Lafayette, LA 70504-3558

Library of Congress Cataloging-in-Publication Data

Names: Wistrand, Carolyn Nur, author.
Title: She danced with a redfish / by Carolyn Nur Wistrand.
Description: Lafayette, LA : University of Louisiana at Lafayette Press,
    2024.
Identifiers: LCCN 2024046432 | ISBN 9781959569183 (paperback)
Subjects: LCSH: Laveau, Marie, 1794-1881--Fiction. | African American
    women--Fiction. | Vodou--Fiction. | Free Black people--Louisiana--New
    Orleans--History--19th century--Fiction. | New Orleans
    (La.)--History--19th century--Fiction. | LCGFT: Biographical fiction. |
    Historical fiction.
Classification: LCC PS3623.I848 S44 2024 | DDC 813/.6--dc23/eng/20241002
LC record available at https://lccn.loc.gov/2024046432

All photos by Cortheal Clark. Cover photo featuring Rashella Mariá as MARIE LAVEAU.

FOREWORD

New Orleans is widely considered one of the most intriguing cities in the United States, and the life and legend of the city's iconic Vodou Queen, Marie Laveau, has played a major role in shaping its mystique. Although New Orleans has been eternalized by the great American playwright Tennessee Williams and numerous films over decades, the perspective of Marie Laveau's own early-nineteenth-century New Orleans community, *les gens de couleur libres* (free people of color), has been under-imagined on both the stage and screen. Cultural amnesia often leads to oblivion and distortion of cultural artifacts, and while Marie Laveau has long been a respected figure in the New Orleans community, she is frequently distorted into an evil character in popular culture, as is the Vodou religion. *She Danced with a Redfish*, written by the award-winning playwright Carolyn Nur Wistrand, a longtime New Orleans resident, creates Laveau's origin story as a young woman struggling with multiple identities. Her play brings to life Laveau's diverse community alongside her personal transformation from the young, devout Catholic wife of a Haitian Revolution immigrant, Jacques Paris, through her journey to become New Orleans's most famous Vodou Queen. In doing so, Wistrand's drama subverts dominant racial narratives told concerning Marie Laveau's time, the segregationist Jim Crow era that followed the Civil War, and the contemporary tendency to sensationalize and vilify both the Vodou religion and Laveau as an agent of horror. Wistrand's drama not only highlights Marie Laveau's story of reclaiming her ancestral traditions, but also, through the multiple characters of *She Danced with a Redfish*, the play presents a nuanced and realistic perspective of the largest community of free people of color in the United States in the nineteenth century, paying respect to how these New Orleanians found ways to thrive in spite of racism, slavery, and the rigid, cruel laws of the Code Noir.

In 1820, the year the play begins, New Orleans had only been a part of the United States for seventeen years and until then had existed for over a century under French and Spanish colonial rule. The New Orleanians depicted in Wistrand's drama are free people of color who were born in New Orleans or recently immigrated during the Haitian Revolution, which ended in 1804. Free people of color in New Orleans enjoyed fragile freedoms under the harsh edicts of the 1724 Code Noir (Black Code) created specifically for the French colony of Louisiana to ensure that White colonists were in control at all levels: social, legal, and economic. Free people of color found guilty of violating this code faced the threat of enslavement, physical violence, and execution. In addition, Catholicism was the mandated religion, and the native religious traditions of Africa and Haiti were forbidden. In New Orleans, African spiritual traditions found expression within Vodou religious practices in various forms of public rituals in places such as in Congo Square or on the banks of Bayou St. John, but they were also practiced in covert, private spaces throughout the city. Marie Laveau was both the Vodou Queen of nineteenth-century New Orleans and a Catholic, which was not as unusual as it sounds. While these identities seem contradictory, this paradox demonstrates the cultural resistance and resilience of New Orleanians of the African diaspora in the face of systematized racism and oppression.

Other nineteenth-century New Orleans icons are characterized in Wistrand's play, such as fellow Vodou practitioners Doctor John (Jean Montanée) and Marie Laveau's mentor and immigrant from Haiti, Sanité Dédé. With Wistrand's addition of the fictional character Colette Delacroix, Marie Laveau's friend, we are granted access to another facet of Laveau's social sphere, namely the quadroon balls. In these balls, young women of color would be paired or "placed" in plaçage, a contractual agreement to be the mistress of a white man, much like a common-law marriage, except many of the men were already married, and this became their second family. Another character in Wistrand's drama, Bras-Coupé, is based on the legendary survivor and fugitive of the Louisiana 1811 Slave Revolt, the largest on United States soil. The cruelty and violence that quelled that revolt and maintained slavery in the South remain a very present threat to the characters in *She Danced with a Redfish*. As such, Wistrand's drama clearly demonstrates the urgency for Marie Laveau to rise as a spiritual leader in her community, which she does by reclaiming the native traditions of her grandmother and ancestors.

Wistrand's play won Southeastern Louisiana University's National Inkslinger Playwriting Competition, and I had the honor of directing *She Danced with a Redfish* at Southeastern's Vonnie Borden Theatre. As a native New Orleanian of French and Spanish Creole descent, I have held a fascination for Marie Laveau since I was a child, so I was thrilled to have the opportunity to present her origin story on our stage in Tangipahoa Parish. My work as a theater artist in New Orleans was very much impacted by the traumatic events following Hurricane Katrina, which taught me the value of creating a stage for untold and under-told stories to reclaim community and sustain and convey cultural memory by making memory literally visible through theater.

One of the unique challenges in bringing Laveau's story to the stage is capturing the colorful locales of the nineteenth-century Vieux Carré—today's French Quarter—with its mix of language, song, dance, and street life. As a director, I felt it necessary to bring the spirit of Congo Square into our production. Congo Square, now part of New Orleans's Louis Armstrong Park, was historically a space where both enslaved people and free people of color congregated one day a week, usually on Sundays, and shared traditional songs, dances, drumming practices, and religious ceremonies of the African diaspora. For our production, our performers trained in African dance and drumming and learned Creole French work songs, festive songs, and lullabies. Wistrand has included in her text ritual chants and physical gestures of the Vodou religion, which we also sought to represent with reverence and accuracy. Although the remnants and legacies of Congo Square are overtly present in the cuisine, jazz, and cultural traditions that define the joy and pride of New Orleans today, those of us working in Wistrand's play made deeper forays to enter this unique reimagining of Marie Laveau's world and characters. My experience working with *She Danced with a Redfish* brought for me an even deeper sense of wonder at Marie Laveau's intelligence, courage, endurance, resilience, and generosity that I carry with me today. As Marie fittingly states in the play's last line: "Even when old bones cover me. The people will remember."

Anne-Liese Juge Fox, PhD
Professor of Theatre
Southeastern Louisiana University
Founding Artistic Director of NOLA Playback Theatre

PRODUCTION HISTORY

She Danced With a Redfish received its world premiere at Cook Theatre, Dillard University, New Orleans in October 2017. The production was directed by David I. L. Poole, with technical director and scenic designer Cortheal Clark, choreography by Jana Meyers-Smith, lighting design by Savion Eagleton, costume design by David I. L. Poole, poster design by Keith Alan Morris, stage managers Dionna Malone and Keserre Hopkins, and master carpenter Robert Weeks. The cast was as follows:

TUESDAY	Sydney Jack
THURSDAY	Jocilyn Johnson
SATURDAY	Loreal Armstead
SANITÉ DÉDÉ	Destani Smith
MARIE LAVEAU	Rashella Mariá
JACQUES PARIS	Zachary Westbrook
BRAS-COUPÉ	Sterling Miller
MARY EARLE	Dominique Lee
DOCTOR JOHN	Khalon Banks
COLETTE DELACROIX	Ariel Lucius
CONGO SQUARE FEMALE DANCERS	Jada Williams, Cierra Brown, Kasey King
CONGO SQUARE MALE DANCERS	Jakari Lister, Elvin Stewart, Jacques Chandler

She Danced With a Redfish premiered on February 19, 2018, at the Vonnie Borden Theatre, Southeastern Louisiana University. The production was directed by Anne-Liese Juge Fox, with technical director and set designer Steven Schepker, lighting design by Benjamin Norman, costume design by Emily Billington, makeup design by Nathaniel Britton, graphic design by Aubree Welton, assistant director Payton Core, and stage managers Jenna Morgan and Amy Schnedia. The cast was as follows:

TUESDAY	Alden Mason
THURSDAY	Sable Diaz
SATURDAY	Breyanna Johnson
SANITÉ DÉDÉ	Shelly Snead
MARIE LAVEAU	Jordin Jones
JACQUES PARIS	Dejuan James
BRAS-COUPÉ	Kennen Gillum
MARY EARLE	Sable Diaz
DOCTOR JOHN	Taylor Larche
COLETTE DELACROIX	Ariel George
UNDERSTUDY	Tyrian Coleman

SHE DANCED WITH A REDFISH

A PLAY IN TWO ACTS

CHARACTERS

Women of Vieux Carré	Chorus (Tuesday, Thursday, Saturday)	20s–40s
Sanité Dédé	Midwife from Saint-Domingue	40s–50s
Marie Laveau	Catholic Creole	20s
Jacques Paris	Carpenter from Saint-Domingue	20s
Bras-Coupé	African Maroon	20s–30s
Mary Earle	Disabled Laundress	20s–30s
Doctor John	African Root Practitioner	30s–40s
Colette Delacroix	Quadroon Creole	20s

TIME AND PLACE

Time:	June 1820–June 1821
Place:	Laveau cottage, St. Ann Street, French Quarter, New Orleans
Settings:	Outside porch, front room, bedroom

ACT I, JUNE 2–8, 1820

Scene 1:	June 2	Friday evening. Outside porch, front room.
Scene 2:	June 2	An hour later. Front room.
Scene 3:	June 3	Saturday morning. Outside porch, front room.
Scene 4:	June 3	A few minutes later. Front room.
Scene 5:	June 3	Saturday evening. Outside porch.
Scene 6:	June 5	A few minutes after midnight. Bedroom.
Scene 7:	June 5	Monday afternoon. Front room.
Scene 8:	June 8	Three days later. Front room, outside porch, bedroom.

ACT II, JUNE 3–23, 1821

Scene 1:	June 3	Sunday afternoon. Front room, outside porch.
Scene 2:	June 4	Monday late morning. Front room, outside porch.
Scene 3:	June 18	Two weeks later. Outside porch.
Scene 4:	June 19	The next day, early evening. Front room.
Scene 5:	June 20	A few minutes after midnight. Bedroom.
Scene 6:	June 21	The next day. Outside porch.
Scene 7:	June 23	Afternoon of St. John's Eve. Front room.

GLOSSARY

Afonga Alafia Ashe Ashe: Literal translation: "Blessings, blessings. I welcome you into my heart." West African welcome song.

Ayido-Weddo: Haitian Vodou goddess, wife of Danbala, known as the rainbow serpent.

Baron Samedi: Haitian Vodou god of the cemetery who is depicted with top hat, sunglasses, smoking a cigar, known for his signature use of profanity when addressing humans.

Bras-Coupé: Literal translation: "Man with one arm." An African American folk hero of New Orleans, the runaway slave that lived in the swamps outside of the French Quarter in the 1800s and escaped death hundreds of times before his final capture.

Bomba hen hen: Literal translation: "It is a secret." Kikongo origins.

Catherine Henry: African maternal grandmother of Marie Laveau.

Code Noir: Translation: Black Code. French edict containing fifty-four articles to regulate slaves and free Blacks in Louisiana established in 1724.

Congo Square: A restricted grassy knoll in the French Quarter where enslaved Africans were allowed to participate in traditional African dancing and drumming every Sunday afternoon in the 1800s. Free people of color also participated in the activities. Jazz historians consider this to be the birthplace of jazz; the modern-day location of Louis Armstrong Park.

Cook: One of the major leaders of the 1811 insurrection in New Orleans. He was captured at Destrehan Plantation and beheaded along with ninety-nine of his compatriots.

Dahomey: African kingdom in West Africa during the 1800s located in modern-day Benin.

Dakodonu: West African King of Dahomey.

Danbala: Haitian Vodou god identified as a serpent spirit.

Deslondes: Charles Deslondes was the leader of the failed 1811 insurrection in New Orleans. He was captured at Destrehan Plantation and beheaded along with ninety-nine of his compatriots.

Doctor John: African free man of color (Jean Montanée) who earned a living as a root doctor in New Orleans, a contemporary of Marie Laveau.

Erzulie Fréda: Haitian Vodou goddess of beauty and love.

Evergreen: A major sugar plantation located outside of New Orleans. Today, it is a working sugar plantation and museum with twenty-seven original slave cabins on the property.

Folkloric Chant to Marie Laveau:
Calinda Calinda (Dance Dance)
Bomba hen Bomba hen (It is a secret)
Eh, ye, ye Mamzelle Marie (Oh, yes, yes, Madam Marie)
Ya, ye ye, li konin tou, gris-gris (She knows well all the powerful magic)
Ay yea, yea Mamzelle Marie, (Oh yes, yes, Madam Marie)
Ya, yea, yea, she knows all the gris-gris (Oh yes, yes, she knows all the powerful magic)
She had gone to school with the old crocodiles
Oh, yes, yea, Mamzelle Marie   (Oh, yes, yes, Madam Marie)
She knows well the Grand Zombi! (She knows well the Grand Spirit Serpent!)

Gede gods: Spirits associated with ancestor worship in Haitian Vodou.

Gris-gris: Amulet worn as a small, concealed bag for protection or to bring harm on an enemy with origins in traditional African religions.

Jacques Paris: A free man of color from Saint-Domingue who married Marie Laveau in St. Louis Cathedral in 1820. He disappeared in 1821; no record of his whereabouts or death have ever been located.

Ju-ju: Amulets or objects used in casting spells in West African witchcraft.

Komina: One of the major leaders of the 1811 insurrection in New Orleans. He was captured and beheaded along with ninety-nine of his compatriots.

Lwa: The primary spirits of Vodou.

Marie Laveau: A free woman of color who was baptized, married by, and had last rites performed by a Catholic priest. Marie was a devout Catholic, hairdresser, and healer. She did not read, write, or give interviews, and signed all documents with an X. It is believed that Marie reigned as the Vodou Queen of New Orleans from 1840–1870. During the nineteenth century, she was vilified and sensationalized as a witch by journalists. In the late twentieth century, female scholars reestablished Marie as a woman who used African traditional practices to empower herself and serve her people. Her tomb in St. Louis Cemetery No. 1 is visited each year by thousands of people.

Maroon: Africans who escaped slavery in the Americas and formed their own settlements.

Ogun: West African Yoruba god of iron.

Papa Legba: Haitian Vodou god, messenger that stands at the crossroads. As the gatekeeper, he is always invoked at the beginning of ceremonies to "open the gate" to procure a channel between the material and ancestral realms.

Père Antoine: Leading Catholic priest in New Orleans in the 1820s.

Place Congo: Original French name for Congo Square.

Sanité Dédé: Mambo priestess. Originally from Saint-Domingue, reputed to be the Vodou Queen of New Orleans in the 1820s.

Shango: West African Yoruba god of thunder.

St. John's Eve: June 23 summer holy day celebration of Vodou devotees in New Orleans.

Tignon: Head wrap worn by Black Creole women. During Spanish rule of New Orleans, Governor Miro proclaimed it to be illegal for any Black Creole woman to appear in public without a tignon.

Vieux Carré: Original French name for the French Quarter.

Vodou: Original Dahomey, West Africa, term for spirit.

Rashella Mariá as **MARIE LAVEAU**

ACT I
Scene 1

Setting: Late evening, June 2, 1820. Outside porch and front room of Laveau cottage, St. Ann Street, New Orleans.

At Rise: *Women of Vieux Carré (Tuesday, Thursday, Saturday), dressed identically in white, are positioned on the porch with baskets filled with sheets, candles, and liquor bottles. Marie, a striking young free woman of color in black dress and mourning veil, faintly appears in the front room kneeling with rosary in front of an altar lit by candles.*

TUESDAY: Sanité Dédé better come on before we get locked up.

THURSDAY: Captain Mazarat is about to be strolling up St. Ann.

SATURDAY: Look at that glow on the moon lighting up the whole street.

TUESDAY: Did you bring the blue candles?

THURSDAY: In my basket with jambalaya.

SATURDAY: I got dirt from Corrachiba's tomb—in case there's trouble.

TUESDAY: Hush. Sanité Dédé said it's got to be tonight.

SATURDAY: You think Marie knows we're out here?

TUESDAY: Hell no.

THURSDAY: Marie is in there saying her rosary like a good Catholic girl.

SATURDAY: Her grandmother never stepped foot in St. Louis Cathedral.

TUESDAY: There was no cross on Catherine Henry's dead body.

THURSDAY: You don't call a priest with Danbala in your belly.

SATURDAY: Marie's grandmother was a powerful woman.

1

TUESDAY: Slept with guinea peppers in her mouth—that's how she bought her freedom.

THURSDAY: Catherine Henry swam back to Africa when she died.

SATURDAY: Shed her skin like a snake.

TUESDAY: Knew the power was in the water.

THURSDAY: They caught Catherine Henry in Dahomey.

SATURDAY: Crossed the Atlantic on the *Dutchman*.

TUESDAY: A big Dane sailor ripped her open.

THURSDAY: Salt water, sperm, and blood rushed up her thighs.

SATURDAY: When that sailor pulled up his pants, Catherine Henry saw past the cross hanging down his neck.

TUESDAY: He shoved her down in the hold chained flat on her back.

THURSDAY: Cross couldn't save him when that sailor started foaming from the mouth.

SATURDAY: Her gods put something fierce on that big Dane.

TUESDAY: All the dark bodies in the hold heard the terror on his tongue before he died.

THURSDAY: They dumped that big Dane sailor in the middle of the Atlantic with three men from Dahomey.

TUESDAY: Catherine Henry saw ninety-nine African gods in the ocean.

THURSDAY: Some were carrying their dead back to Africa.

SATURDAY: And some were traveling with the chained black gold— coming to America.

WOMEN OF VIEUX CARRÉ: Bomba hen hen!

(Sanité Dédé, a powerful midwife from Saint-Domingue, walks up. Picking up an empty plate behind the steps, she turns to the women.)

SANITÉ DÉDÉ: Bras-Coupé?

WOMEN OF VIEUX CARRÉ: Empty.

(Sanité Dédé conceals the plate, walks up the steps, and knocks. Marie opens the door.)

SANITÉ DÉDÉ: We've come to cleanse the house.

MARIE: Sanité Dédé, it's almost midnight.

SANITÉ DÉDÉ: You knew we were coming. You dressed for it.

(Sanité Dédé and Women of Vieux Carré enter with baskets.)

MARIE: I can't sleep. First time I been alone since Jacques and I were married.

SANITÉ DÉDÉ: You said he was coming back Sunday.

MARIE: That's what I'm hoping. Two White men pulled up in a wagon. Said they were hiring carpenters out at Evergreen. I don't even know where that is.

SANITÉ DÉDÉ: Evergreen is a mean plantation out on the German Coast. He better watch himself—they're likely to put him out in the sugarcane.

MARIE: Don't say that—Jacques is a free man.

SANITÉ DÉDÉ: He's just Black hands that "got away" to those planters.

MARIE: You are stressing me out.

SANITÉ DÉDÉ: It should be done tonight, before your Jacques Paris returns.

MARIE: Right. You're right . . .

SANITÉ DÉDÉ: Is it so difficult to honor her traditions?

MARIE: I'm just nervous.

SANITÉ DÉDÉ: Spirit is on all sides, Marie.

MARIE: Jacques is so against it.

SANITÉ DÉDÉ: I didn't come for your husband. You opened the door.

MARIE: I've been praying for ma mère's soul.

SANITÉ DÉDÉ: Good. Say your rosary. But learn of the spirit as your grandmother knew it.

MARIE: I won't break my promise to her.

SANITÉ DÉDÉ: Bring the pink candle from the Virgin. Lay out your plates on the bedsheets. These spirits are hungry.

(Women of Vieux Carré, take bedsheets, candles, and food out of baskets, arranging them across the floor. Candles are lit at each corner of the room. Sanité Dédé pours a libation in each corner of the room. Sounds of African drums are heard. Women of Vieux Carré form a circle and begin to gyrate. Marie stands at altar holding a pink candle.)

You should never hear the spirit without standing at the gate. *(Knocking on the ground.)* Papa Legba open the gate.

WOMEN OF VIEUX CARRÉ: Papa Legba let her pass.

SANITÉ DÉDÉ: She died on Tuesday. *(Blindfolding Tuesday with a strip of white cloth.)*

TUESDAY: Claim her from the North.

SANITÉ DÉDÉ: We laid her out on Thursday. *(Blindfolding Thursday with a strip of white cloth.)*

THURSDAY: Claim her from the South.

SANITÉ DÉDÉ: They put her in a tomb on Saturday. *(Blindfolding Saturday with a strip of white cloth.)*

SATURDAY: Claim her from the East.

SANITÉ DÉDÉ: Nine months she's been swimming the ocean. Claim her from the West, Marie.

(Marie moves into the circle. Sanité Dédé blindfolds Marie with a strip of white cloth and pours a libation in the center of the bedsheets. Sounds of African drums intensify. Women of Vieux Carré continue to gyrate. Marie trembles.)

WOMEN OF VIEUX CARRÉ: Eh! Eh! Bomba hen hen.

SANITÉ DÉDÉ: Danbala open the sky.

(Thunder erupts, intermingling with African drums.)

MARIE: "Blessed art thou among women and blessed is the fruit of Thy womb. Pray for our sins now and at the hour of death."

WOMEN OF VIEUX CARRÉ: The hour of death.

SANITÉ DÉDÉ: The hour of death.

(As the women intensify their gyrating dance, Jacques Paris, a solidly built young man, enters with toolbox, taking in the spectacle.)

JACQUES: *(Enraged)* Marie?

MARIE: Jacques?

(Jacques rips blindfold off Marie. Drums are silenced.)

JACQUES: What the hell have you done to my wife?

(Stillness permeates the room.)

Somebody better say something.

SANITÉ DÉDÉ: You know what this is.

JACQUES: I sure as hell know what this is. But what I don't know is why you got the nerve to bring this evil shit into my house.

SANITÉ DÉDÉ: Your house?

JACQUES: That's right. You know it is against the law.

SANITÉ DÉDÉ: Don't speak of the White Man's Code Noir. You were set free on Saint-Domingue. How do you forget the *power* that broke Napoleon's sugarcane?

JACQUES: We living in America, Sanité Dédé. You better get your mind straight.

SANITÉ DÉDÉ: How many slave cabins that planter paid you to build out at Evergreen?

JACQUES: Get out of my house, you goddamn bitch.

SANITÉ DÉDÉ: You slap the Face of God with your mouth. Be careful.

JACQUES: Don't threaten me, old woman. I'll take your black cat and wrap its tail around your ugly neck if I ever catch you or any these of these filthy witches up inside my house again. Now take your baskets of dead bones and get out of here. All you whores—get out!

SANITÉ DÉDÉ: You bring trouble into this house.

(Jacques storms into the bedroom. Marie broods in the middle of the room. Sanité Dédé and Women of Vieux Carré gather their belongings in silence as Bras-Coupé, an African maroon, appears from behind the porch. He

is a dangerous figure with wild locks of hair, alligator teeth hanging from his bare chest, and raggedy pants made from strips of animal hide. Sanité Dédé and Women of Vieux Carré leave the house.)

SANITÉ DÉDÉ: (*To the women*) Get home. I'll contact you.

(Women of Vieux Carré walk down the street. Sanité Dédé senses the presence of Bras-Coupé.)

(Sotto voce) Bras-Coupé?

(Bras-Coupé throws a feather tied to the shell of a crawfish on the porch but remains out of her view.)

I knew you would show up. We got Creoles in this city licking off a mule's ass. That Jacques Paris in there is one of them.

(Bras-Coupé places the empty plate on the steps. Sanité Dédé takes a piece of fried fish from her basket, places it on the empty plate.)

There will be a full plate by my door if you make it over to Rampart Street.

(Sanité Dédé leaves. Bras-Coupé grabs plate. The moon lights up his strange presence. Startled, he disappears. The lights fade.)

Rashella Mariá as **MARIE LAVEAU** and
Zachary Westbrook as **JACQUES PARIS**

ACT I
Scene 2

Setting: An hour later. Front room of Laveau cottage.

At Rise: *Marie, still brooding, sits in rocking chair. Jacques, in night pants, comes out of the bedroom.*

JACQUES: Marie, come to bed.

MARIE: I am not ready to lay down with you, Jacques.

JACQUES: You are my wife. You sleep in my bed.

MARIE: Your wife, your house, your bed.

JACQUES: Don't be mad at me for protecting you. There ain't a man in New Orleans that wants his wife dancing with Sanité Dédé and her witches.

MARIE: They sure knock down her door when it's their woman's time. Sanité Dédé has delivered more babies than any midwife in this quarter.

JACQUES: I'll give her that.

MARIE: Sanité Dédé is the queen. Everyone bows before her on Place Congo.

JACQUES: And who goes out there?

MARIE: Half the city.

JACQUES: City slaves and field slaves—that's who is out there when she smears chicken blood up her dress on Sunday afternoon. You ain't gonna see no free man of color with his woman out on Congo Square.

MARIE: That is not true. My grandmother was a free woman. And she went out there every Sunday.

JACQUES: She wasn't always free. Besides she was African, that's why she was still one of them.

MARIE: Listen to what you are saying! All my grandmother asked of me was one small ritual cleansing nine months after she passed. And you took that from her tonight.

JACQUES: I never agreed to it. You should have told me what you was planning before I left.

MARIE: And then what? For God's sake, Jacques, you tried to throw Sanité Dédé out of here when my grandmother was dying.

JACQUES: I told you to send for Père Antoine.

MARIE: But she wasn't Catholic.

JACQUES: She was in our house.

MARIE: Go to bed, Jacques.

JACQUES: I've been held up in the back of a wagon all day trying to get back here to you. How am I supposed to sleep with my wife sitting out here dressed for a funeral? Forget about it. Come to bed.

MARIE: I just can't.

JACQUES: I am sorry if I upset you. I mean that. But that shit puts me on edge.

MARIE: I was trying to respect my grandmother's faith.

JACQUES: Listen to me, this goes all the way back to Eve. She ate from that tree, and it turned her into a damned snake. When you take a power that wasn't made for humans, the soul starts to disappear. I saw it on Saint-Domingue. It is nothing to play with.

MARIE: You were a small boy during a revolution.

JACQUES: And I know what went on! Men drinking blood from the neck of a goat like it was milk from their mother's nipples; women getting down on all fours turning the Virgin Mary upside down on a Catholic altar. It's bad ju-ju.

MARIE: You were born on the island that had the power to drive out the French, Jacques.

JACQUES: Don't romanticize what happened on that island. Toussaint L'Ouverture was the real hero of the revolution. And they let him rot to death in a French prison. I came to America as a free man to walk into the future. That means I got to do business with the White man—not think up ways to slit his throat when he is sleeping. I'm done with revolution.

MARIE: There is one coming.

JACQUES: What's that supposed to mean?

MARIE: Every time I pass that slave pen on Commons, the smell is enough to knock me down. I can't bear to look at greased, Black bodies on display like butcher meat two blocks from my house. I don't know when. I don't know how. But a revolution is coming.

JACQUES: You better be careful what comes out of your mouth.

MARIE: It doesn't bother you that so many of our people are enslaved?

JACQUES: You are my people. Nobody else. I didn't make this country— I'm trying to survive in it.

MARIE: So it doesn't bother you?

JACQUES: Of course it bothers me. You take a blind man. Yeah, I feel bad for him. But that doesn't mean I am supposed to cut out my eye and give it to him.

MARIE: If I could do something, I would.

JACQUES: But that's just it—you can't. When I saw them burning sugar out at Evergreen . . . damn . . . those fields smelled like Saint-Domingue. There is a Black man inside of me that could have picked up a hammer and brought it down on the head of any one of those White planters. Don't think the thoughts aren't there. But I got to look to the end of things. We need food on this table and money to pay for the taxes on this house. I am trying to keep you safe.

MARIE: It wasn't right what you did tonight. You really hurt me.

JACQUES: I didn't mean to. It's been a hard week, I am exhausted.

MARIE: Please go over to Sanité Dédé's house in the morning and apologize.

JACQUES: I can't believe that just came out of your mouth.

MARIE: That front door has to be open to her.

JACQUES: Did you even listen to anything I just said?

MARIE: She has never lost a baby, Jacques.

JACQUES: What are you saying—you pregnant?

MARIE: That's what I am thinking.

JACQUES: You're hitting me hard.

MARIE: I need her here with me in the morning. She will know.

JACQUES: Come to bed.

MARIE: Are you going to make it right with Sanité Dédé? Even Madame Vauclain called for Sanité Dédé when she went into labor. She is the best midwife in the Quarter, and everyone knows it. I won't have anybody else touching my body.

JACQUES: I heard you.

(Jacques undresses Marie. She is a sight of beauty in a white camisole with raven locks of luminous hair.)

MARIE: Sanité Dédé has to be the one to deliver my child.

JACQUES: All right, if that is what you need, I'll make it right with her. I love you, Marie. And it's more than you know.

(Jacques picks up Marie and carries her into the bedroom. The lights dim.)

Khalon Banks as **DOCTOR JOHN**

ACT I
Scene 3

Setting: Saturday morning. June 3, 1820. Outside porch and front room of Laveau cottage.

At Rise: *Doctor John, a formidable African root practitioner, with scarification marks on both cheeks, sporting a black coat with tails, sits on the outside porch. Mary Earle, a disabled laundress walking with a severe limp, approaches with her basket.*

MARY EARLE: I need to get up those steps.

DOCTOR JOHN: Plenty of room.

MARY EARLE: If you get off them.

DOCTOR JOHN: Sun is barely up and you limping down the street like you been on your feet all day. But then you was up half the night waiting on your man to come home.

MARY EARLE: Who are you?

DOCTOR JOHN: The one they call the Doctor.

MARY EARLE: Yeah, I heard about you.

DOCTOR JOHN: I could help you.

MARY EARLE: You out on Bayou Road?

DOCTOR JOHN: I got something keep John Earle under your covers all night.

MARY EARLE: How you know all my business?

DOCTOR JOHN: It's my job to know who is messing up, who needs assistance . . . you gonna come and see me?

15

MARY EARLE: Maybe so—if you let me get up these steps.

(*Doctor John moves out of her way. Mary Earle knocks on door. Marie opens door. Mary Earle enters.*)

MARY EARLE: Got your sheets soft as cotton, Madame Marie.

MARIE: Set them on the table.

(*Mary Earle sets down the basket on the table.*)

There is nothing like sleeping on clean sheets with your man.

MARY EARLE: You are starting to fill out. Marriage suits you.

MARIE: You think?

MARY EARLE: A man don't like no skinny woman that feels like dead bones to the touch.

MARIE: What's going on with you, Mary Earle?

MARY EARLE: I'm just saying, a man don't like no skinny woman— especially if she crippled.

MARIE: Was John Earle out all night?

MARY EARLE: Pretty much.

MARIE: I'm sorry.

MARY EARLE: John Earle don't seem to be able to hang on to steady work. That's what keeps him out half the night. Is that the rest of this load?

MARIE: Yes. (*Pulling a pair of pants out of the basket*) I don't know what he got on these pants.

MARY EARLE: Looks like some kind of grease. I'll get it out.

MARIE: *(Placing coins in Mary Earle's hand)* Can you have these back by Monday?

MARY EARLE: I'll be here.

(Mary Earle walks over to door. Doctor John knocks on door.)

MARIE: That should be Sanité Dédé.

(Mary Earle opens door. Doctor John walks in.)

DOCTOR JOHN: Marie Laveau.

MARY EARLE: He was on your steps when I came up.

(Doctor John gestures for Mary Earle to leave.)

DOCTOR JOHN: Take care of that leg, Mary Earle.

(Mary Earle walks out.)

I am here to pay my respects. I knew your grandmother.

MARIE: My grandmother passed nine months ago.

DOCTOR JOHN: These things take time.

MARIE: I am not dressed to receive a stranger.

DOCTOR JOHN: Jean Montanée is no stranger to the women of this house.

MARIE: My grandmother?

DOCTOR JOHN: And your mother. I guess she doesn't come around that much now that she is the mistress of Charles Laveau.

MARIE: Thank you for paying your respects.

DOCTOR JOHN: The people need a queen.

MARIE: You're at the wrong door.

DOCTOR JOHN: You will be on the throne. It's written on your forehead.

MARIE: This is making me uncomfortable.

DOCTOR JOHN: I can read you, Creole girl, from the bottom of your feet to the top of your head.

MARIE: You need to leave.

DOCTOR JOHN: *(Grabbing Marie's palm)* XXX. This X is Jacques Paris—your husband—the carpenter from Saint-Domingue that turned his back on the power.

MARIE: *(Pulling her hand back)* Stay away from me!

DOCTOR JOHN: Go make up the bed with those clean sheets for your husband. Enjoy it. Jacques Paris will die to you in one year.

MARIE: Get out!

DOCTOR JOHN: I'll see you next year.

(Doctor John walks out as Women of Vieux Carré appear on Marie's steps.)

TUESDAY: Doctor John is a no-good hoodoo man.

THURSDAY: Makes his living off the palm of his hand.

SATURDAY: Fortune-telling and gris-gris all in his game.

DOCTOR JOHN: I first smelled my manhood in Cuba.

TUESDAY: A cook in Cuba can earn a fortune

THURSDAY: Even a slave . . .

SATURDAY: If he can spice with peppers.

DOCTOR JOHN: Bought my freedom from that Cuban and walked out of the swamp with a crocodile.

WOMEN OF VIEUX CARRÉ: Dressed up like the Cuban Plantation Man!

DOCTOR JOHN: But I don't cook pepper pot soup for no White man!

(Doctor John offers his arm to the Women of Vieux Carré and they stroll out. Marie stands braced against the door staring at her palm.)

Rashella Mariá as **MARIE LAVEAU**
and Ariel Lucius as **COLETTE DELACROIX**

Setting: A few minutes later. Outside porch and front room of Laveau cottage.

At Rise: *Marie hasn't moved from the door. Colette Delacroix, a light-skinned Creole woman, overly dressed for the day, walks up the steps and knocks. Marie doesn't respond. Colette knocks again.*

COLETTE: Marie! It's Colette.

MARIE: Colette. Is there anybody else out there?

COLETTE: No. There is no one. Look.

MARIE: Get in here and close the door.

COLETTE: Are we still going to the market, or did you forget?

MARIE: You didn't see a man out there when you came up?

COLETTE: What strange man is paying *you* a visit this early in the morning?

MARIE: Stop—this is serious.

COLETTE: What happened?

MARIE: I don't want to put the words out there. I won't repeat it.

COLETTE: You better tell Jacques as soon as he gets home.

MARIE: No! I just want to get his bad energy off me.

COLETTE: Well, you are no fun. I guess you want to ruin my whole day.

MARIE: I am sorry, I am not good company this morning.

COLETTE: I don't want to go alone. Please.

MARIE: Colette. I can't. I barely got any sleep last night. Honestly, I feel nauseous. Jacques came home late. And this ugly man that just came by—I am afraid we will run into him.

COLETTE: Well, for God's sake, who is he? You can at least tell me that.

MARIE: Jean Montanée.

COLETTE: Isn't he the one they call Doctor John? That conjure man with tattoos across his face?

MARIE: Have you seen him before?

COLETTE: I have. He is scary. They say he can read the future. What was that man doing over here?

MARIE: You didn't pass him on the street?

COLETTE: No. Tell me what he said.

MARIE: Don't ask. Aren't you a little fancy for the market?

COLETTE: If you want to be on the arm of a captain, wouldn't you need to be a little fancy?

MARIE: French or American?

COLETTE: French! Captain LaCour . . .

MARIE: Married or single?

COLETTE: Too many questions, Marie. If you won't come to the market, at least fix my headdress.

MARIE: Sit down.

COLETTE: I can never tie it straight. I hate that we have to cover our hair in public. My mother said Spanish women demanded the law.

MARIE: I don't know the history of it.

COLETTE: French women would never be so jealous in their demands. The sight of blue-black hair flowing down the backs of cream and coffee Creoles has unsettled too many supper tables.

MARIE: Free or slave, the custom demands we cover our hair.

COLETTE: We shouldn't be bound by an old Spanish law. They are not worn at the masked balls.

MARIE: What?

COLETTE: It is true. If you hadn't married a carpenter, you would know.

MARIE: Even before Jacques, I never wanted to be on display.

COLETTE: It is not like that. The entire room lined in purple iris and magnolia. The most delicate oysters slip through your tongue until a gentleman takes your hand. And when he does, there is no tignon on your head that marks you.

MARIE: It is an exhibition. You are being paraded around.

COLETTE: You have never been, so you don't get an opinion.

MARIE: No Frenchman that goes to a masked ball is looking for a wife.

COLETTE: Don't make it sound so vulgar.

MARIE: But it is.

COLETTE: Is your mother the wife of Charles Laveau?

MARIE: No.

COLETTE: And is he your father?

MARIE: Yes.

COLETTE: Then don't cast stones.

MARIE: *(Handing Colette a mirror)* I just want you to be happy.

COLETTE: You should be a hairdresser, Marie. You've turned my tignon into a beauty statement. *(Beat.)* Don't be so upset.

MARIE: I am sick to my stomach.

COLETTE: Tell Jacques what that bastard Doctor said so he can go beat the hell out of him.

MARIE: And then what? He might put something on Jacques.

COLETTE: You and your damn superstitions. Ever since we were little, if you weren't saying a rosary at Mass you'd be lighting a candle at the altar. Tell me you don't still sleep with all those Catholic saints around your neck?

MARIE: They protect me.

COLETTE: Then why are you so freaked out by what that man said?

(Sound of someone knocking at door.)

Let me answer it! If it's that son of a bitch, I'll get rid of him. *(Opening door.)* It's Sanité Dédé.

MARIE: I was praying you'd come.

SANITÉ DÉDÉ: Mademoiselle Delacroix. Madame Paris.

MARIE: Please sit with me.

SANITÉ DÉDÉ: Why is Collette dressed for dinner before noon?

COLETTE: It is the fashion, Sanité Dédé. This looks like it is going to get serious. Well, let me go. I should get to the market before the sun ruins my face.

SANITÉ DÉDÉ: Watch yourself.

COLETTE: *(Kissing Marie on the cheek)* I hope you feel better.

MARIE: Come by next Monday and I will go to the market with you.

COLETTE: Promise?

MARIE: Promise.

COLETTE: It was good to see you Sanité Dédé.

SANITÉ DÉDÉ: Mademoiselle.

    (Colette departs.)

MARIE: I am so sorry about last night.

SANITÉ DÉDÉ: When you beat a man, the body heals. When you curse a man, it clings on the shadow of the soul.

MARIE: How can that be?

SANITÉ DÉDÉ: The soul is spirit—it travels between worlds.

MARIE: Forgive Jacques—and me.

SANITÉ DÉDÉ: This room is heavy . . . it needs to be scrubbed out.

MARIE: *(Dry heaving)* Oh God . . . I think I am going to vomit . . .

    (Sanité Dédé takes bucket from altar.)

SANITÉ DÉDÉ: Here.

    (Marie vomits in bucket.)

MARIE: I've been nauseous all morning.

SANITÉ DÉDÉ: Clean yourself. Jacques said you might be with child. *(Cupping her hands on Marie's stomach.)* When was your last period?

MARIE: March. I had a few spots of blood in April, but it was only for a day.

SANITÉ DÉDÉ: April, May, June—you are three months pregnant.

MARIE: Are you sure?

SANITÉ DÉDÉ: There is life in your womb.

MARIE: This is what I have been praying for, to make things right between me and Jacques.

SANITÉ DÉDÉ: Your baby should be here by December. You have to get through this summer heat. Clean yourself standing up—no dirty water near the vagina, that could kill the baby. Eat five fruits a day—but no apples, they harm the kidneys. You are only allowed meat once a week. Mark the day.

MARIE: Jacques likes his beef twice a week, sometimes three.

SANITÉ DÉDÉ: Put fish on his plate. Beef hardens the umbilical cord and makes birthing more difficult. Your breasts are going to fill out by the end of August. In November, I will prepare a salve for your nipples— you want them hard when your milk comes in. When is the last time he made love to you?

MARIE: This morning early.

SANITÉ DÉDÉ: No more sex. You could hurt the baby.

MARIE: We can't make love until December?

SANITÉ DÉDÉ: You don't let that man get between your legs until the first of the year. Your body has to heal. You only spotted that one time?

MARIE: Yes, I thought I was starting my period but then it stopped. Sanité Dédé, would you read my hand?

SANITÉ DÉDÉ: So there is something else in this room. What happened?

MARIE: Do you know Jean Montanée?

SANITÉ DÉDÉ: I do.

MARIE: Did he know ma mère? Does he know my mother?

SANITÉ DÉDÉ: He does.

MARIE: He was here. This morning.

SANITÉ DÉDÉ: Why did you open your door to him?

MARIE: He said Jacques would die to me in one year! He said it was on my hand!

(Sanité Dédé examines Marie's hand.)

SANITÉ DÉDÉ: He marked you.

(Sanité Dédé searches room with urgency.)

MARIE: It can't be true.

SANITÉ DÉDÉ: There is gris-gris in this house. We have to find it.

MARIE: He was only here a few minutes.

SANITÉ DÉDÉ: Jean Montanée will disappear standing in front of you. Check the corners. Under the table. Behind the altar.

(Marie and Sanité Dédé search the room for gris-gris.)

MARIE: I didn't let him in. Mary Earle opened the door. I thought it would be you.

SANITÉ DÉDÉ: It's in the laundry basket.

(Marie and Sanité Dédé shake out sheets. Sanité Dédé pulls out a small bag of gris-gris.)

MARIE: In between my clean sheets.

SANITÉ DÉDÉ: Trying to get next to your skin.

MARIE: Those are my wedding sheets.

SANITÉ DÉDÉ: You have to break the spirit he brought in this room. Burn them.

MARIE: Jacques and I made love the first time on those sheets.

SANITÉ DÉDÉ: Never lay down on them again. This has to be destroyed.

MARIE: Will you do it, please?

SANITÉ DÉDÉ: *(Opening gris-gris bag)* Goofer dust, cat bones. What's this he's got wrapped up in hair? *(She unties the tiny object.)*

MARIE: God, it's an eye! Is it human?

SANITÉ DÉDÉ: No—some kind of animal. Maybe a dog.

MARIE: Why is he doing this?

SANITÉ DÉDÉ: What else was on his tongue?

MARIE: *(Touching her forehead)* Something about my forehead.

SANITÉ DÉDÉ: He has been looking for a woman to reign with him.

MARIE: You are the queen!

SANITÉ DÉDÉ: Montanée knows better than to approach me. That is why he marked you.

MARIE: I don't want anything to do with him.

SANITÉ DÉDÉ: Cut this open. It will keep Montanée from entering your
    dreams.

MARIE: *(Dry heaving)* Oh God—here it comes again . . . *(Marie vomits.)*

SANITÉ DÉDÉ: *(Handing Marie a cloth)* You should go lie down.

MARIE: Look at these sheets—all soft and white, full of dirt. What if he
    tries to harm my baby?

SANITÉ DÉDÉ: Light nine candles in this room for a week. Five blue,
    four black. Scrub the floor with vinegar before you lay down salt in the
    corners. When does Jacques get in?

MARIE: He comes in around six on Saturday.

SANITÉ DÉDÉ: When will he go to bed?

MARIE: After his dinner, about ten.

SANITÉ DÉDÉ: Is he a light sleeper?

MARIE: No, he sleeps hard.

SANITÉ DÉDÉ: You make sure he is sleeping hard. Get up an hour before
    midnight. If he is still awake, tell him you got to relieve yourself. *(Taking
    bottle out of apron.)* Mix seven drops of this oil with your pee . . .

MARIE: Sanité Dédé . . .

SANITÉ DÉDÉ: Seven drops for seven days. That's protection for the
    whole week. Mix the oil with your waste and sprinkle it down the steps
    outside. Shouldn't take you more than five minutes. It's got to be done
    before midnight. Tomorrow morning, go out there and shake those
    steps down with brick dust. *(Placing bottle in Marie's hand.)* Take it.

MARIE: I hope I can remember all that.

SANITÉ DÉDÉ: Nine candles—five blue, four black. Salt the corners of this room after you've scrubbed the floor with vinegar. Seven drops of that oil mixed with your pee on the front steps before midnight. Tomorrow morning, put down brick dust out there.

MARIE: My stomach feels bad. This room is spinning.

SANITÉ DÉDÉ: Do as I tell you and Jean Montanée will break his neck the next time he tries to come up your steps. I'm taking these sheets and dead bones out of here.

MARIE: Are you sure you have to burn my wedding sheets?

SANITÉ DÉDÉ: Tuesday, Thursday, and Saturday will be on the porch with three black candles before midnight. When they blow out those candles, it is your time.

(*Lights crossfade to outside porch.*)

ACT I
Scene 5

Setting: Saturday evening of the same day, June 3, 1820. Outside porch of Laveau cottage.

At Rise: *Women of Vieux Carré linger on front steps holding black candles.*

TUESDAY: Doctor John's snake has gone all around this house, I can feel it.

THURSDAY: He sure brought some trouble up here on St. Ann Street.

SATURDAY: He ain't walking with Sanité Dédé's power.

TUESDAY: Don't be so sure—Doctor John's got some wicked magic.

THURSDAY: You think these black candles will keep him away?

SATURDAY: Sanité Dédé dipped them in rooster blood.

TUESDAY: Doctor John put something on us this afternoon.

THURSDAY: You think?

SATURDAY: That's why she sent us back out here.

TUESDAY: We are burning that man's sweat off our flesh.

THURSDAY: You couldn't wait to be on Doctor John's arm, Tuesday.

SATURDAY: You were the one rolling your eyes, Thursday.

TUESDAY: Who was the one swishing their behind up in his face when we turned up Royal Street?

THURSDAY: She told the truth, Saturday. That was you.

SATURDAY: They say Doctor John got fifteen wives out on Bayou Road.

TUESDAY: I heard he is doing business with two Frenchmen on Bourbon Street.

THURSDAY: What about the one-eyed, one-legged German woman with no tongue?

SATURDAY: You think it's true? You think he got a White woman out there?

TUESDAY: If he does she is a hag that crawled out of the bayou.

THURSDAY: His serpent got a fierce bite.

SATURDAY: Doctor John gets in the circle with three candles on his head.

TUESDAY: Only a queen wears the crown on Lake Pontchartrain!

WOMEN OF VIEUX CARRÉ: Bomba hen hen!

(Women of Vieux Carré blow out candles and quickly disappear. Marie opens front door with chamber pot.)

MARIE: Seven drops on each step? What did she say? Blessed Virgin. What am I doing? Jacques is going to smell my piss on these steps. This is crazy.

(Bras-Coupé throws a feather tied to the shell of a crawfish on the porch but remains out of view. Marie dumps chamber pot on the side of the porch, splashing Bras-Coupé.)

Oh my God! Who is out here?

(Bras-Coupé comes into view wiping his face.)

BRAS-COUPÉ: Hush.

MARIE: What are you doing behind my porch?

BRAS-COUPÉ: Waiting.

MARIE: Did Doctor John send you out here to kill me?

BRAS-COUPÉ: No one sent me. No one speaks for me. No one owns me.

MARIE: Who are you?

BRAS-COUPÉ: Bras-Coupé.

MARIE: The African maroon? There's a reward out on you.

BRAS-COUPÉ: Nine years.

MARIE: You been in the swamps all those years?

BRAS-COUPÉ: Deslondes, Cook, Komina—they were three. In the swamp, the talk was revolution. Then others joined. There were enough Africans on the German Coast to take out the sugar planters. Cook hacked François Trépagnier into pieces. His blood baptized the shout, "Freedom or death." Halfway to the city, militia surrounded us at Destrehan. I made it to the swamp. When I came out . . . their heads were on poles, all down River Road back to the center of the Vieux Carré. One hundred African heads on poles.

MARIE: I saw those heads when I was too small to remember. Ma mère covered my eyes. Those poles lined this quarter a long time. We don't speak of it.

BRAS-COUPÉ: Next June I will beat the drum for Deslondes, Cook, Komina in Congo Square.

(Jacques's voice is heard from inside.)

JACQUES: Marie.

(Bras-Coupé taps Marie's forehead with crawfish feather.)

BRAS-COUPÉ: Kill my name in the day, but feed me at night.

(Bras-Coupé disappears as Jacques steps out on porch.)

JACQUES: Why you out here?

MARIE: I was nauseous, needed fresh air. Didn't mean to wake you.

JACQUES: What is that—the chamber pot?

MARIE: Couldn't stand the smell of it in our room.

JACQUES: Why did you dump it out here in front? You should have taken it out back.

MARIE: I forgot.

JACQUES: You ain't natural.

MARIE: What do you mean?

JACQUES: Could be the pregnancy, or those grimy sheets on the bed. You usually change them on Saturday.

MARIE: We'll have clean sheets on Monday.

JACQUES: I gave you money to pay Mary Earle this morning.

MARIE: She is going through a bad time.

JACQUES: Smells like swamp water out here. Come on. Let's go inside.

(*Marie turns back to catch a glimpse of Bras-Coupé as Jacques leads her inside. Jacques and Marie cross the front parlor into the bedroom and climb in bed.*)

JACQUES: (*Kissing Marie*) Try to get some sleep.

MARIE: You too.

(*Blackout.*)

ACT I
Scene 6

Setting: A few minutes after midnight, June 4, 1820. Bedroom in Laveau cottage.

At Rise: *Melting colors of a dream state bleed into the room. Jacques and Marie are asleep. Women of Vieux Carré, in identical red dresses, dance into the room and circle the bed with a sheet.*

WOMEN OF VIEUX CARRÉ:
Kiss the tongue at midnight
that turns into a snake.
Let the hair of Erzulie
cross bones at Legba's gate.
Wander in a dream state
until you disappear.
Marriage vows are broken
when the Saturday god appears.

(Women of Vieux Carré drop the sheet. Doctor John, dressed as the Haitian lwa, Baron Samedi, smoking a cigar in top hat, black tails, and sunglasses, sits upright in the bed holding Marie.)

DOCTOR JOHN: *(Puffing on a cigar)* That carpenter dropped his seed but now he got to roll over.

(Doctor John flicks cigar ashes on Jacques.)

MARIE: Wrap your snake across my neck.

DOCTOR JOHN: All right, bitch—if you bring me some rum.

MARIE: No problem.

(Marie pulls a bottle of rum from behind the pillow. Doctor John takes a drink as he wraps the snake across Marie's neck.)

How do I look?

35

DOCTOR JOHN: Like the smell of death . . . sweet.

MARIE: Who's got to die?

DOCTOR JOHN: It's on your hand.

MARIE: So it is, Baron Samedi.

DOCTOR JOHN: Came down yesterday to get Catherine Henry's bones, and this son of a bitch you married sent her back to graveyard dirt. Took me nine months to carve that casket.

MARIE: Just kill him so I can sleep with the snake.

DOCTOR JOHN: Why are humans so damn impatient? Death takes time—especially when it is cursed.

(Marie stands on the bed.)

MARIE: *(Kicking Jacques)* Why didn't you ride the donkey backward out at Evergreen, you stupid ass?

(Jacques twists and turns in his nightmare.)

DOCTOR JOHN: Throw him out so I can make love to you.

MARIE: Get out of my bed, carpenter!

(Marie kicks Jacques again; he drops to the floor.)

DOCTOR JOHN: Only take five minutes to dig his grave.

MARIE: Saturday is yours, Baron Samedi.

(Doctor John and Marie begin to embrace. Jacques jumps up.)

DOCTOR JOHN: You heard your wife. Saturday is mine. Don't lift that ugly human head. Get back down on the floor.

(Doctor John throws his arm out. Jacques gasps from strangulation and falls to the floor. The room vibrates with strange drum sounds. Women of Vieux Carré circle Jacques.)

WOMEN OF VIEUX CARRÉ:
You can't lift your arm.
You can't lift your head.
Lie down and be comfortable.
The snake is in your bed.

(Drums rise as Women of Vieux Carré swirl around the room. Jacques, fighting his troubled subconscious, grasps the corner of the bed.)

JACQUES: Get off my wife, gravedigger.

(Doctor John embraces Marie.)

DOCTOR JOHN: Your husband got no respect for the dead. You pissed off the Gede gods, island man.

TUESDAY: When the spirits are hungry, set down a plate.

THURSDAY: When the spirits are thirsty, bring two bottles of rum.

SUNDAY: When Papa Legba stood at the crossroads, *you* closed the gate.

(Women of Vieux Carré swirl out of the bedroom with sheet.)

JACQUES: Where you going with our wedding sheet? Bring that back.

DOCTOR JOHN: Get me something to eat, woman.

(Marie jumps up and pulls a plate of chicken and rice from under the bed. Doctor John smokes, drinks, and eats on the bed as Marie dotes over him. Jacques looks on in horror.)

JACQUES: Marie belongs to me!

DOCTOR JOHN: Shut up with that tired old song. Human girls like to dance across the river on Saturday night.

(Sanité Dédé appears.)

SANITÉ DÉDÉ: The people of Saint-Domingue remember her gods.

JACQUES: I don't want those memories in the belly of my wife.

SANITÉ DÉDÉ: You don't decide who the gods claim at midnight! Who was the little boy in Saint-Domingue that brought Erzulie Fréda flowers and perfume? Don't turn your head, you know it's true.

JACQUES: I ain't thinking about that evil spirit.

SANITÉ DÉDÉ: Erzulie Fréda taught you how to love a woman you couldn't own.

JACQUES: Wearing three wedding bands for her three snake husbands.

SANITÉ DÉDÉ: But every Thursday she takes a human man. How many times did she take you, Jacques Paris?

JACQUES: I don't know—I can't remember.

SANITÉ DÉDÉ: You shaved your head so she could ride you—all the way from Saint-Domingue to Dahomey.

JACQUES: I don't pray to that water witch in America.

SANITÉ DÉDÉ: The water between Saint-Domingue and New Orleans is here, Jacques. You are drowning in it.

(Jacques physically struggles in his dream. Marie wakes up. Doctor John jumps off bed, wraps the snake around his neck and walks through the walls of the room. Sanité Dédé vanishes. Marie shakes Jacques.)

MARIE: Jacques, wake up!

JACQUES: Bitch, don't touch me.

MARIE: Jacques!

(Jacques sits up and stares at Marie.)

JACQUES: I know where you been—and who you been with.

MARIE: Stop dreaming. Wake up!

JACQUES: I got to go to work.

(Jacques gets out of bed and dresses.)

MARIE: In the middle of the night?

JACQUES: Where is my boots?

MARIE: You planning to go out on the street half naked?

JACQUES: Don't try to keep me from my job.

MARIE: You don't work tomorrow.

JACQUES: What?

MARIE: Tomorrow is Sunday. We are going to nine o'clock Mass.

JACQUES: You ain't fit to stand before a priest and take communion.

MARIE: Are you talking to me?

JACQUES: I knew that snake was going to find me. You just couldn't leave it alone.

MARIE: For God's sake, would you wake up!

JACQUES: I am awake! I can see you.

MARIE: What do you see?

JACQUES: I don't know.

MARIE: You are scaring me, Jacques.

JACQUES: You got any rum behind that pillow?

(Jacques reaches behind Marie's pillow looking for rum then grabs her hair and smells it.)

MARIE: What are you doing?

JACQUES: Smelling your hair. There is no cigar smoke on it, but that gravedigger was in this bed. *(Looking under bed)* Where is that plate of chicken you gave him?

MARIE: You're inside your own nightmare. Please come out of it, Jacques. Nobody has been in this bed. I swear that on the Blessed Virgin.

JACQUES: Are we still married?

MARIE: Of course we are. You the only man I have ever been with. I am carrying your child.

JACQUES: I've been fighting the devil in my own graveyard.

MARIE: You had a bad dream, Jacques.

JACQUES: It was real.

MARIE: All the fears of the day came back to haunt you, but it is over.

JACQUES: Someone was trying to strangle me—take you from me.

MARIE: Talk to Père Antoine after Mass this morning.

JACQUES: What is he going to do? This ain't got nothing to do with the Catholic Church. Just forget it—I am all right now.

MARIE: Do you think you can go back to sleep?

JACQUES: I am just going to sit here for a while.

MARIE: I love you.

JACQUES: Uh-huh.

MARIE: Did you hear me?

JACQUES: Close your eyes and pray you don't dream.

(Marie and Jacque are silent as the lights dim.)

Dominique Lee as **MARY EARLE**
and Rashella Mariá as **MARIE LAVEAU**

ACT I
Scene 7

Setting: Monday afternoon, June 5, 1820. Outside porch and front room of Laveau cottage.

At Rise: *Marie is scrubbing floor in front room on hands and knees. Colette is sitting at table taking feathers and ribbons out of a basket. Mary Earle approaches front steps but is stopped on the corner by Jacques, who begins to rummage through her basket.*

MARY EARLE: You are about to mess up all those clothes I just folded, Jacques Paris.

JACQUES: There's no sheets in here.

MARY EARLE: I got that grease out of your pants, look for yourself.

JACQUES: You were paid to bring clean sheets on Saturday.

MARY EARLE: And I brought them.

JACQUES: When?

MARY EARLE: Always bring Miss Marie clean sheets on Saturday.

JACQUES: Not last Saturday.

MARY EARLE: What you talking about? Your wife put her hands on them.

JACQUES: You swear it?

MARY EARLE: They was in the basket, I am telling you.

JACQUES: Something ain't right.

MARY EARLE: Maybe that man stole them.

JACQUES: What man?

43

MARY EARLE: That conjure man that was hanging around.

JACQUES: Who you talking about?

MARY EARLE: Doctor John.

JACQUES: Jean Montanée—the witch doctor out on Bayou Road? You telling me he was in my house on Saturday?

MARY EARLE: I don't remember.

JACQUES: What you mean you don't remember? You just said he was here.

MARY EARLE: Miss Marie didn't say anything about it?

JACQUES: *(Grabbing her arm)* My wife said you were going to bring clean sheets on Monday.

MARY EARLE: I don't want any trouble.

JACQUES: Was Jean Montanée in my house on Saturday?

MARY EARLE: He was out here on your steps when I brought the laundry.

JACQUES: And she let him inside?

MARY EARLE: It wasn't like that.

JACQUES: Is that the only time you have seen him over here?

MARY EARLE: Yes.

JACQUES: Keep your mouth shut about this.

(Jacques takes off down the street.)

MARY EARLE: Wait! I was the one that opened the . . . door. Lord God. If it ain't one kind of trouble, it is something else.

(Mary Earle struggles up the steps with the weight of the world on her back and knocks. Marie rises and opens the door.)

MARIE: Be careful when you come in. The floor is still wet.

MARY EARLE: You can smell that vinegar.

COLETTE: Keep that front door open, get some fresh air in here.

MARY EARLE: I got the grease out of his pants.

MARIE: *(Taking laundry basket)* Great.

COLETTE: *(Holding up two feathers)* Which one would go better with my green dress?

MARIE: The pink one. I need to ask you something, Mary Earle.

MARY EARLE: I'm listening.

MARIE: You know the sheets you brought on Saturday?

MARY EARLE: They were in the basket when I left! You put your hands on them, Miss Marie.

MARIE: I am not accusing you, Mary Earle.

COLETTE: Are you sure about this pink one?

MARY EARLE: I am just saying I don't know nothing about those sheets.

COLETTE: It might be a little too pink against the green. Maybe I should add a ribbon.

MARIE: I need another pair just like them.

MARY EARLE: Why? What happened?

COLETTE: *(Holding up a feather)* Maybe this white one with the gold thread?

MARIE: They were a gift—my wedding sheets.

MARY EARLE: You can pick those up on the corner of Toulouse and Burgundy.

COLETTE: I told you it was that shop on Toulouse.

MARY EARLE: They will cost you—at least two silvers—but that man has got the best French linen in the Quarter.

MARIE: Perfect. There is a half a load by the door.

MARY EARLE (*Picking up basket*): I will have this back on Saturday.

COLETTE: Is anybody going to say anything about this white feather?

MARY EARLE: Miss Marie, you forgot to pay me.

MARIE: Forgive me, here.

MARY EARLE: Appreciate you.

(*Mary Earle leaves. Marie sprinkles salt in corners.*)

COLETTE: Oh, I forgot about the gold lace! Wouldn't this be stunning with the white feather?

MARIE: Just let me finish in here so we can head over to that shop. I can't even think straight.

COLETTE: That is because you let Sanité Dédé burn those damn sheets.

MARIE: Don't say another word, Colette.

COLETTE: You are not going to shut me up—I am your best friend.

MARIE: It is done.

COLETTE: Why didn't you tell Jacques in the first place? This is turning into the nightmare from hell.

MARIE: You think I don't know it? All day Sunday he just sat out on the porch. He didn't even kiss me goodbye when he went to work this morning.

COLETTE: He will get over it as soon as you get those sheets on the bed.

MARIE: God, I hope so.

COLETTE: Do you even have enough money to buy another pair?

MARIE: I've been holding back a little from what he gives me on Saturday.

COLETTE: That is exactly why I am not going to get married. Once you sign that piece of paper, you have to beg for a dime.

MARIE: No, you are just going to lay down with a man that belongs to somebody else and pray he drops a quarter on his way out.

COLETTE: Now you are being a bitch—and you still haven't told me what you think of this gold lace.

MARIE: It is lovely. No one is going to come up in my house and take Jacques from me.

COLETTE: Just let your vinegar and salt do their magic.

MARIE: Are you ready? I also need to pick up blue and black candles.

COLETTE: Of course you do.

MARIE: We have to be back here by four.

COLETTE: Maybe this black lace on the sleeves and bodice of the green dress?

MARIE: Let's go, Colette. I need those sheets on my bed before Jacques gets home from work.

(*Marie and Colette walk out and stroll down the street.*)

Sterling Miller as **BRAS-COUPÉ**

ACT I
Scene 8

Setting: Thursday evening, June 8, 1820. Front room, outside porch, bedroom of Laveau cottage.

At Rise: *Marie is visibly anxious as she resets the silverware, looks at the food, crosses to the altar, lights candles, walks around adding more salt in the corners, then surveys the room.*

MARIE: Where could he be?

> *(Marie walks out on the porch looking down the street. Women of Vieux Carré pass the house.)*

WOMEN OF VIEUX CARRÉ: Evening, Marie.

MARIE: Evening.

TUESDAY: You out here awful late.

THURSDAY: Sure is a beautiful night.

SATURDAY: Except for that gray cloud across the moon.

TUESDAY: Heard you was expecting.

MARIE: December.

THURSDAY: A Christmas baby.

SATURDAY: You let us know you need anything.

MARIE: Have you seen Jacques up that way?

TUESDAY: Sure haven't.

THURSDAY: Haven't seen him all week.

SATURDAY: Is he still working over on Iberville?

MARIE: I am not sure.

TUESDAY: If we see him, we'll tell him you are waiting on him.

MARIE: He hasn't come home.

SATURDAY: For how long?

MARIE: Three days. I haven't seen him since Monday.

TUESDAY: And he knows you are expecting a child?

THURSDAY: He shouldn't be leaving you alone for three days.

MARIE: I am about ready to go out of my mind.

TUESDAY: Maybe he went back out to Evergreen.

MARIE: He would have told me.

SATURDAY: When those White men pull up, you got to get in the wagon.

TUESDAY: I know that is right.

THURSDAY: You check with his family?

MARIE: Jacques doesn't have family here. Things haven't been right since
     last Friday.

SATURDAY: Men get that way. He is just trying to cool off.

MARIE: I have been up and down the Vieux Carré looking for him.

THURSDAY: Fix yourself some chamomile tea.

MARIE: I couldn't keep it down—my nerves are bad.

THURSDAY: You have to take care of that baby.

TUESDAY: Sanité Dédé know about this?

MARIE: I'm going over there tomorrow.

THURSDAY: You want her to come and sit with you?

MARIE: Maybe so.

SATURDAY: You shouldn't be going through this alone.

MARIE: Nobody has seen him.

TUESDAY: Sanité Dédé will take care of it.

THURSDAY: She'll find him.

SATURDAY: Go in there and get off your feet.

TUESDAY: Working yourself up ain't going to help.

SATURDAY: Put some brick dust on those steps in the morning.

TUESDAY: You don't know who is coming up these streets.

(*Women of Vieux Carré stroll up the street. Marie walks back into the house.*)

MARIE: How could I forget to put out the brick dust?

(*Taking a broom and bowl of brick dust outside, Marie hears a rattling sound in back of porch.*)

Oh God, now what?

(*Bras-Coupé throws a crawfish tied to a feather on the porch.*)

Bras-Coupé, is that you back there?

BRAS-COUPÉ: I need to eat.

MARIE: Hold on, I got food going to waste inside.

(Walking back inside, Marie fixes a plate, grabs a spoon and napkin, takes it out and sets it down on the corner of the steps.)

Here.

(Bras-Coupé takes the plate, puts spoon and napkin back on the steps.)

That's stew meat—you need the spoon.

BRAS-COUPÉ: Bitter.

MARIE: My stew?

BRAS-COUPÉ: This meat is loaded with salt.

MARIE: It is called seasoning.

BRAS-COUPÉ: Your hand was too heavy when it stirred the pot.

MARIE: Mix it up with that rice—

BRAS-COUPÉ: Is the street clear?

(Marie walks down the steps and looks down the street.)

MARIE: There is no one out here.

BRAS-COUPÉ: Get back up those steps. Don't look at me.

MARIE: You should say something nice about the food on that plate. It is my husband's favorite dish. I paid good money for that meat.

BRAS-COUPÉ: You made this for him?

MARIE: I've cooked that dish for the last three nights. I just sit in there waiting.

BRAS-COUPÉ: A carpenter knows where his wife sleeps.

MARIE: My husband could be dead.

BRAS-COUPÉ: There are worse things than death.

MARIE: I agree. Like how I feel right now.

BRAS-COUPÉ: *(Coming out of the shadows wiping his face, staring at Marie)* You are holding power.

MARIE: Don't say that! This whole shitting mess started with Jean Montanée saying that.

BRAS-COUPÉ: Montanée sleeps with a crocodile that bites—be careful.

MARIE: I don't even know that man.

BRAS-COUPÉ: The spirit is here at this house. It will find you.

MARIE: I need to find my husband, Jacques Paris. He hasn't been home in three days.

BRAS-COUPÉ: A queen of the village sees a trace in the dust. Track him.

(Bras-Coupé touches Marie's forehead).

MARIE: *(Startled)* What are you doing?

BRAS-COUPÉ: Blessing your gift. Don't be afraid of the eye in back of your forehead.

MARIE: I am Catholic.

BRAS-COUPÉ: A Catholic woman with second sight.

MARIE: Why do you keep coming over here?

BRAS-COUPÉ: You must carve my secrets on your skin.

MARIE: I can't do that.

BRAS-COUPÉ: The memory of our people is in your blood.

MARIE: I am carrying my husband's child, and something has happened to him. I can feel it.

BRAS-COUPÉ: Every mark on your hand holds a sorrow you shouldn't speak.

MARIE: We are at the crossroads.

BRAS-COUPÉ: You don't hear spirit without standing at the gate.

MARIE: You escaped.

BRAS-COUPÉ: I had a wife, but I never laid down with her. The sky opened up and I ran.

(Bras-Coupé slips out.)

MARIE: So, you are going to leave? Is that what all men do? *(Sweeping steps and sprinkling brick dust)* Can't even see to put this down. *(Gazing at the night sky)* Is that a road opening up across the moon? I am starting to see footsteps. Jacques Paris, are those your feet on that road? Where are you going off to? You got to turn around. Can you hear me out there? Turn around.

(Marie loses her balance and falls down steps. She lays face down on the bottom of the steps, slowly forcing herself up the steps, leaving the door wide open as she struggles to light a candle at the altar. Looking down at her skirt, she smells blood.)

Oh God, no—please God no. Blessed Virgin, is this blood? Uh.

(Marie collapses in a chair. Sanité Dédé appears on the front steps. Seeing the front door open, she steps inside and closes the door.)

SANITÉ DÉDÉ: He left the city.

MARIE: I can't hear you. *(Placing hands across her stomach)* Uh. Jesus.

SANITÉ DÉDÉ: What is wrong?

MARIE: I am in pain. Terrible.

SANITÉ DÉDÉ: Where?

MARIE: My stomach. I am bleeding.

SANITÉ DÉDÉ: When did it start?

MARIE: Just now. I fell out on the steps.

SANITÉ DÉDÉ: Let's get you on the bed.

    (Sanité Dédé and Marie cross into the bedroom. Sanité Dédé tears back coverlet and top sheet, assisting Marie onto the bed.)

MARIE: *(Excruciating pain)* Oh my God.

SANITÉ DÉDÉ: Sit up and spread your legs.

    (Sanité Dédé sits on the side of the bed examining Marie.)

MARIE: Is there more blood?

SANITÉ DÉDÉ: How hard did you fall?

MARIE: Down to the bottom step. *(Hit by a painful contraction)* Uh.

SANITÉ DÉDÉ: We have to stop this blood.

    (Sanité Dédé crosses out to front room to retrieve bucket.)

MARIE: Am I going to lose the baby? Where are you going?

SANITÉ DÉDÉ: Stay calm.

MARIE: Oh God, make it stop.

(Sanité Dédé returns with bucket of water and grabs top sheet.)

SANITÉ DÉDÉ: Got to tear this up.

(Sanité Dédé bites into corner of top sheet, tearing it into pieces and soaking sheet in water.)

MARIE: I'm scared.

SANITÉ DÉDÉ: Keep breathing.

MARIE: I can't take this pain.

SANITÉ DÉDÉ: Ride with it.

MARIE: Blood is coming out like water.

SANITÉ DÉDÉ: Then let it come. *(Cleaning Marie with sheet)* Pink mucus.

MARIE: Is that a good sign?

SANITÉ DÉDÉ: You are almost there.

MARIE: *(Expelling fetus)* I can't take any more. Uh.

(Sanité Dédé wraps dead fetus in the top sheet.)

What are you doing?

SANITÉ DÉDÉ: Lay down. We have to get your uterus to contract.

MARIE: Is that my baby in there?

SANITÉ DÉDÉ: Stay still before you bleed to death.

(Sanité Dédé rubs down Marie's uterus.)

It was never meant for this earth.

MARIE: What are you saying?

SANITÉ DÉDÉ: Your baby wasn't strong enough to make it in this world.

MARIE: Let me see it.

SANITÉ DÉDÉ: No.

(Marie pushes Sanité Dédé aside and unwraps sheet.)

MARIE: Look at that little bloody face. But there are no fingers or feet—it looks like a piece of liver.

SANITÉ DÉDÉ: *(Wrapping sheet over dead fetus)* This is nature, cleansing the body.

MARIE: *(Climbing out of bed)* Let me hold it.

SANITÉ DÉDÉ: You are still bleeding. That baby is dead.

MARIE: *(Holding the dead fetus)* Before you take my child, Blessed Virgin, let this baby know how much love was here, waiting.

SANITÉ DÉDÉ: Marie, you are in shock. Give it to me.

MARIE: Jacques won't ever hold our child.

SANITÉ DÉDÉ: Get on this bed before you bleed out.

MARIE: You are a Christmas baby who came in June. Your papa is Jacques Paris. A free man from Saint-Domingue. I am your mother, Marie Laveau. You were born free. Let my baby know that, Blessed Virgin.

(Blackout.)

Destani Smith as **SANITÉ DÉDÉ**

ACT II
Scene 1

Setting: One year later, Sunday afternoon, June 3, 1821. Front room in Laveau cottage

At Rise: *Marie is seated in a rocking chair. Sanité Dédé walks up the steps with a basket of roots and knocks. Marie ignores the sound. Sanité Dédé opens the door and walks in.*

SANITÉ DÉDÉ: You been to Mass?

> *(Marie rocks with a blank gaze in her eyes.)*

It is a beautiful June Sunday. Come with me to Place Congo. Let the drums put some heat back in your blood.

MARIE: I am waiting on my husband.

SANITÉ DÉDÉ: You need to get out of that chair.

MARIE: Jacques has been coming to me in dreams. I can smell him, wrapped inside my hair.

SANITÉ DÉDÉ: It takes seven years to get a man's sex off a woman's spirit. Start today.

MARIE: I don't want to get him off me. I want to feel him on me.

SANITÉ DÉDÉ: You are not the first woman to lose a man. I've got no sorry to give you.

MARIE: He was part of my soul.

SANITÉ DÉDÉ: You had him for a year. Some people don't get a day.

MARIE: I lost Jacques and my baby in three days.

59

SANITÉ DÉDÉ: And you buried that baby a year ago. It's time you do the same to Paris. You can't bring him back.

MARIE: Can you?

SANITÉ DÉDÉ: Do you want a man in your bed that don't come natural?

MARIE: Yes—maybe I do.

SANITÉ DÉDÉ: Snap out of it, girl.

MARIE: Jacques is never coming back?

SANITÉ DÉDÉ: It has been a year, Marie, and not one word. For all he knows, you are out on the streets searching for scraps to feed that baby. He left you and his child. What's it going to take for you to bury his ass and move on?

(Women of Vieux Carré and Mary Earle come up the street with Bras-Coupé lying naked, a cloth across his buttocks, covered in a net, on a two-wheeled wooden laundry cart. Tuesday rushes up steps and barges into Marie's front room.)

TUESDAY: We got Bras-Coupé out here. He has been calling for you, Marie.

SANITÉ DÉDÉ: What do you mean, you got Bras-Coupé?

TUESDAY: White men got him in Congo Square. They took him to the Cabildo and cut him up. Dumped his body out on the bricks just now.

(Sanité Dédé hurries outside, Marie stands holding her stomach.)

SANITÉ DÉDÉ: No men came to help you?

TUESDAY: Plenty of them was waiting by the prison gate.

THURSDAY: Doctor John stood out there the whole time.

SATURDAY: In the shadows.

SANITÉ DÉDÉ: What the guard say when you took him?

TUESDAY: Bastard pointed his rifle at our breasts, said, "Get this runaway African nigger out of here."

MARY EARLE: The mens loaded him in my cart.

SATURDAY: That White man was ready to lock up every Black man on the street. Better we came alone.

MARY EARLE: His blood has already soaked up three loads of my wash.

(Marie walks out on steps.)

SANITÉ DÉDÉ: We need to get him inside. Marie?

MARIE: Of course, bring him in.

SANITÉ DÉDÉ: *(To Marie)* Need your hands.

(The women attempt to lift the wagon up the steps.)

MARY EARLE: My leg is about ready to give out.

SANITÉ DÉDÉ: Marie trade places with Mary Earle. All right. Steady . . . it is just three steps.

(The women lift the wagon up the steps. Bras-Coupé moans in agony as they roll the wagon into the front room.)

Close those curtains—I don't want people looking in here.

MARIE: *(Closing curtains)* There is no one out there.

SANITÉ DÉDÉ: I can feel them . . . waiting. *(Examining the body)* We got to cut this off him. Get my knife out of the basket.

(Tuesday hands Sanité Dédé a knife. Women of Vieux Carré surround the cart.)

What happened?

TUESDAY: Police caught him dancing in broad daylight out on Congo Square.

THURSDAY: Jumped in the circle with alligator teeth hanging down his neck!

SATURDAY: Everybody went crazy. That's what brought the police out there.

TUESDAY: Those White men came up on all sides—they was quick.

(Bras-Coupé continues to let out agonizing sounds as Sanité Dédé cuts the net from his body. Women of Vieux Carré roll back the net.)

THURSDAY: One threw this net on him. Rest of them beat him to the ground.

SATURDAY: Dragged Bras-Coupé to the prison.

TUESDAY: They got an evil room in the calaboose for African runaways.

THURSDAY: When they were done carving him up, they threw his body out on the bricks.

SATURDAY: They wasn't even trying to bury him.

SANITÉ DÉDÉ: Why did you come this June Sunday, Bras-Coupé? Why did you come in the day?

BRAS-COUPÉ: Ahhh . . .

SANITÉ DÉDÉ: The rest of our tomorrows we got to smell your blood on these streets, you fool.

MARY EARLE: You think he'll make it to morning?

SANITÉ DÉDÉ: Go home, Mary Earle. Put your leg up and soak it soon as you get in.

MARY EARLE: Just need to rest it for a while.

SANITÉ DÉDÉ: Watch yourself tonight.

MARY EARLE: I'll come by tomorrow for my cart.

MARIE: The smell of blood is strong in here.

(Sanité Dédé takes roots, oil jars, and bundle of cloth from her basket.)

SANITÉ DÉDÉ: Papa is coming for Bras-Coupé. Look at him and hold the memory. Soak up that blood.

(Women of Vieux Carré apply cloths to Bras-Coupé's bleeding body as Sanité Dédé prepares a salve with roots and oils.)

MARIE: Mother of God, his ears . . .

TUESDAY: Sliced from his head.

THURSDAY: Bras-Coupé is a graveyard of flesh.

SATURDAY: His story is with the Africans that put it in their minds to burn the sugar plantations.

TUESDAY: One hundred Black heads on poles. This one escaped.

THURSDAY: Nobody knew when he would come to the Vieux Carré.

SATURDAY: As long as Bras-Coupé was breathing free in the swamps, those White men might wake up with their throats slit.

TUESDAY: But now he danced in Congo Square this June Sunday.

MARIE: Will he die?

SANITÉ DÉDÉ: Dahomey birthed him too fierce to break—Papa coming for him tonight. Marie, bring your bowl from the altar.

(Marie hands her the bowl.)

Drain this African's blood in the bowl.

(Women of Vieux Carré wring out blood into bowl.)

MARIE: In the name of the Father, the Son . . .

SANITÉ DÉDÉ: Put the cross behind you. There is only spirit here.

MARIE: He needs prayer!

SANITÉ DÉDÉ: *(Applying roots to the bleeding body)* Papa coming to take him home . . . oh I can feel him coming. You gonna witness something tonight, Marie!

MARIE: I would pray to the Blessed Virgin for his soul.

SANITÉ DÉDÉ: You don't have the memory of where Africans go when the drum stops.

MARIE: Only Jesus Christ can save his soul.

SANITÉ DÉDÉ: A Creole woman got to do more than lick the White man's muscle.

MARIE: You mustn't say that.

SANITÉ DÉDÉ: Sanité Dédé see this. She decide. *(Spits in cloth)* Those Americans put the net on this leopard. Look—see how they cut the tendons from his knees.

MARIE: Ugly. I hate them for it.

(Sanité Dédé pours a libation around the wooden cart.)

SANITÉ DÉDÉ: Too much blood.

(Sound of African drumming comes up.)

WOMEN OF VIEUX CARRÉ: Drumming!

SANITÉ DÉDÉ: They can't stop the drum when Papa is coming.

(The women sense the spirits of the Ancestors entering the room .)

MARIE: Something just came in the room.

SANITÉ DÉDÉ: *(Taking bottle of rum from basket)* Place this on the altar—they gonna be thirsty. Papa Legba, you got the keys. Open the gate. Open the door. Who is going to come to take him home?

(Sanité Dédé knocks on the ground three times. Women of Vieux Carré kiss the ground three times.)

BRAS-COUPÉ: Marie.

SANITÉ DÉDÉ: Kneel down, he wants to speak.

(Marie kneels down next to Bras-Coupé. He whispers in her ear.)

BRAS-COUPÉ: Dakodonu.

MARIE: Dakodonu? What does that mean?

SANITÉ DÉDÉ: His African name. We got to wash him.

(Women of Vieux Carré assist Sanité Dédé in washing the body.)

WOMEN OF VIEUX CARRÉ: *(Chanting)*
Dakodonu is African. We got to wash him clean.
Dakodonu is African. We got to wash him clean.
Dahomey in his belly. Birth him at the shore.
Now they call him back.

BRAS-COUPÉ: Get me a walking stick.

SANITÉ DÉDÉ: The door is open, and he is passing through. He needs a cane to step over. Give him a stick—anything.

(Women of Vieux Carré rush around the room looking for a stick.)

That broom.

(Tuesday places broom in Bras-Coupé's hands.)

MARIE: Holy Mary, Mother of God, pray for our sins now and at the hour of our death.

SANITÉ DÉDÉ: *(Tearing a piece of cloth with her teeth)* Put this between your legs.

MARIE: What?

SANITÉ DÉDÉ: Do it!

(Terrified, Marie places the cloth between her legs. Bras-Coupé, with supernatural strength, sits up on the cart, then uses the broom to stand.)

WOMEN OF VIEUX CARRÉ: He is rising!

MARIE: Dakodonu?

(Bras-Coupé walks with broom toward Marie.)

MARIE: Oh God . . . he is coming out of his skin. He is walking into me.

(Bras-Coupé drops broom stick and thrusts both hands onto the stomach of Marie transferring the power. She stands transfixed by pleasure and pain as the power penetrates her.) Ah!

BRAS-COUPÉ: *(Blessing Marie)* Ashe Ashe.

WOMEN OF VIEUX CARRÉ:
Ashe Ashe.
Afonga Alafia Ashe Ashe.

(Women of Vieux Carré chant in a counterclockwise circle around Bras-Coupé and Marie.)

SANITÉ DÉDÉ:
> Our gods traveled with us
> Before the sugarcane
> slave ship
> Door of No Return.
> This house remembers her gods.

(Drums rise. Sanité Dédé removes outer dress from Marie. In an altered state, Marie begins to dance. Women of Vieux Carré continue to chant in counterclockwise circle.)

WOMEN OF VIEUX CARRÉ:
> Ashe Ashe.
> Afonga Alafia Ashe Ashe.

MARIE: Water is rushing through me . . . piercing me with cool liquid . . . I am inside the black of the blue ocean . . .

SANITÉ DÉDÉ: You standing with it; now you must die and resurrect to walk inside it.

MARIE: I am drowning.

BRAS-COUPÉ: Let me smell my sacrifice in this room. Bring the bowl.

WOMEN OF VIEUX CARRÉ:
> Ashe Ashe.
> Afonga Alafia Ashe Ashe.

(Sanité Dédé brings bowl containing his blood, Bras-Coupé offers his blood to Sanité Dédé, who drinks from the bowl, passes it to Women of Vieux Carré to drink, then hands bowl to Marie.)

BRAS-COUPÉ: Taste the spirit of Ogun.

(Marie brings the bowl to her lips and drinks.)

WOMEN OF VIEUX CARRÉ:
> Ashe Ashe.
> Afonga Alafia Ashe Ashe.

WOMEN OF VIEUX CARRÉ: Kasey King, Jocilyn Johnson, Cierra Brown, Loreal Armstead, Sydney Jack, Jada Williams; Destani Smith as **SANITÉ DÉDÉ**; Rashella Mariá **MARIE LAVEAU**; Sterling Miller as **BRAS-COUPÉ**

BRAS-COUPÉ: This is finished.

(Bras-Coupé drops to the floor, dead.)

SANITÉ DÉDÉ: Stand back!

MARIE: Dakodonu is swimming with the First Ancestor . . . I can see him, crossing the ocean.

SANITÉ DÉDÉ: Where is he going, Marie?

MARIE: *(Falling to floor)* Africa.

SANITÉ DÉDÉ: The power is alive in New Orleans.

(Blackout.)

ACT II
Scene 2

Setting: The next day, June 4, 1821. Front room of Laveau cottage.

At Rise: *The body of Bras-Coupé has been removed. Sanité Dédé sits at table. Marie remains on the floor.*

SANITÉ DÉDÉ: These people up and down the street whisper with coiled tongues. Can you hear them?

> *(Marie does not respond. Sanité Dédé rises, takes bucket, and pours water on Marie.)*

Get up.

MARIE: My head is spinning.

SANITÉ DÉDÉ: Take your time.

MARIE: Feel terrible . . .

SANITÉ DÉDÉ: Show me your eyes. You know where you are?

MARIE: In my front room . . . there is blood on my lips.

SANITÉ DÉDÉ: *(Handing Marie a cup of tea with valerian root)* Drink this.

MARIE: Where is he?

SANITÉ DÉDÉ: They took his body early.

MARIE: Mother of God—what is going on inside of me?

SANITÉ DÉDÉ: It is nothing bad.

MARIE: It feels like this room is at the bottom of the ocean.

SANITÉ DÉDÉ: You don't crawl on your belly to enter the sacred circle. You have to grow into it.

MARIE: He put a thousand secrets in my soul. I don't understand any of this, Sanité Dédé.

SANITÉ DÉDÉ: Gifts come from the spirit. You were born with it. Did you bleed that first time with Jacques?

MARIE: I can't remember.

SANITÉ DÉDÉ: Was there blood on the sheet the first night Jacques made love to you?

MARIE: No.

SANITÉ DÉDÉ: Is it your monthly?

MARIE: No. I had my period last week.

SANITÉ DÉDÉ: Give me the cloth under your skirt. You put it there last night.

MARIE: *(Lifting her chemise and removing the cloth)* There is blood on it. That can't be.

SANITÉ DÉDÉ: Sanité Dédé knows how to read it. In Saint-Domingue, Old Marie was one with the First Ancestor.

MARIE: You scare me.

SANITÉ DÉDÉ: Swear on this cloth there was no blood on the sheet the first time you and Jacques made love.

MARIE: I won't put my hands on it. Throw it out.

SANITÉ DÉDÉ: This blood is sacred. Swear you are telling me the truth.

MARIE: Why do you keep asking? I've told you.

SANITÉ DÉDÉ: Then, it is as his blessing. You belong to the First Ancestor. Dakodonu bled you.

MARIE: That can't be.

SANITÉ DÉDÉ: You don't decide. The Ancestors chose you. They can be terrible—heal or kill. You must learn to stand in the spirit and honor them.

(Mary Earle comes up steps and knocks. Sanité Dédé opens door.)

MARY EARLE: I come for my cart. Everybody is talking about Bras-Coupé out there. *(To Marie)* You all right?

SANITÉ DÉDÉ: She had a rough night—we all did.

MARY EARLE: This cart smells like rum.

SANITÉ DÉDÉ: You can't put laundry baskets on his blood. I had to clean it.

MARY EARLE: Is it safe?

SANITÉ DÉDÉ: It will bring you luck if you don't let John Earle drink up your money.

MARY EARLE: Going to need your help getting it down those steps.

(The three women roll the cart out the door.)

SANITÉ DÉDÉ: Marie and I will take it down, Mary Earle.

MARY EARLE: You sure?

SANITÉ DÉDÉ: Wait down there.

(Sanité Dédé and Marie take the cart down the steps.)

MARY EARLE: I will come by on Saturday. Hope you be feeling better.

(Mary Earle rolls cart down the street. Doctor John strolls up.)

DOCTOR JOHN: I heard you ladies had quite a night.

SANITÉ DÉDÉ: You have no business with us, Jean Montanée.

DOCTOR JOHN: Where did they take his body?

SANITÉ DÉDÉ: You got an eye in back of your forehead. Don't come here asking questions.

DOCTOR JOHN: People say they brought his body to a young woman last night. Say he was calling for Marie Laveau. Is that true?

SANITÉ DÉDÉ: Careful.

DOCTOR JOHN: *(To Marie)* I asked you a question. Was Bras-Coupé calling your name before he died?

SANITÉ DÉDÉ: His blood is still fresh.

DOCTOR JOHN: Why is she standing out here on the steps in a night slip with her eyes glazed over?

SANITÉ DÉDÉ: Marie is Catholic.

DOCTOR JOHN: I am asking her. You possessed, girl?

MARIE: You've got alligators crawling on your face.

DOCTOR JOHN: These are scarifications of a Senegalese prince. I am the pure blood of Africa, vexed mulatress. I serve the spirit.

SANITÉ DÉDÉ: No! You serve lies you feed up to the people. Doctor John, a Senegalese prince? I should go out there and tell them who you are: a Cuban slave that makes pepper pot soup.

DOCTOR JOHN: This bitter memory has dried you up.

SANITÉ DÉDÉ: One hundred African men with their heads cut off! Charles Deslondes, Komina, Cook—your brothers. You knew.

DOCTOR JOHN: You can't stop a Black man's rage in the heat of revolution. They took a blood oath. I said it would fail. They didn't have the guns or the backup, surrounded by French slave planters and American militia. No escape but the bayou swamp.

SANITÉ DÉDÉ: Those heads picked apart by vultures.

DOCTOR JOHN: I have the memory too.

SANITÉ DÉDÉ: These ten years, Bras-Coupé been in them swamps . . . the people had something.

DOCTOR JOHN: But now he is dead. The people need a new queen.

SANITÉ DÉDÉ: It is not enough, what you give them?

DOCTOR JOHN: I am just getting started in this city.

SANITÉ DÉDÉ: You make people sick then sell them the cure.

DOCTOR JOHN: I am running a business. What you doing?

SANITÉ DÉDÉ: Sanité Dédé doesn't use the power to sell goods in the market.

DOCTOR JOHN: You think the paper that says you are a free woman smells like a peach ripe for picking? The man that put ink on your paper has got more power than Jesus Christ when he takes out his money at the slave pens. Jean Montanée will use his power to walk free in this city and they will call me Doctor.

SANITÉ DÉDÉ: Don't even try to come up these steps.

DOCTOR JOHN: She is going to be the queen in New Orleans, old woman. Not you.

MARIE: Stay away from me!

DOCTOR JOHN: It has already been decided and there is not a damn thing either one of you witches can do about it. I read it on her hand. You better learn your trade, girl.

(Doctor John strolls down the street. Marie and Sanité Dédé walk back in the house and lock the door.)

MARIE: He took Jacques from me, that evil bastard.

SANITÉ DÉDÉ: Don't give him that much power. He is just a bridge you have to walk over.

MARIE: I can still smell his blood . . . Dakodonu.

SANITÉ DÉDÉ: You remember Bras-Coupé's African name. Good. It will make you strong.

MARIE: I'm breaking down. Dying.

SANITÉ DÉDÉ: The part of you that was with Jacques Paris is ready to die.

MARIE: His X is branded on my soul.

SANITÉ DÉDÉ: Marie has more than one X on her hand.

MARIE: How can life change so much in one day?

SANITÉ DÉDÉ: You came when the drums called. *(Touching Marie's hair)* This hair carries power you got to learn to walk in. Teach you a trade. No queen waits on a man to make groceries.

MARIE: Jacques is still here on the ends of my hair, but now—all of a sudden—it smells like yesterday.

SANITÉ DÉDÉ: *(Taking scissors from her apron and handing them to Marie)* The present holds past and future. Cut off the last year.

MARIE: I don't know if I am strong enough.

SANITÉ DÉDÉ: Let him die so you can bury him, Widow Paris. You walk in bones and flesh a short time.

(Marie takes the scissors, grabs the ends of her hair and cuts as the lights go down.)

ACT II
Scene 3

Setting: Two weeks later, June 18, 1821, late evening. Outside porch of Laveau cottage.

At Rise: *Women of Vieux Carré are positioned on the porch with baskets and lit candles.*

THURSDAY: Feels like we are the police, sitting out here every night for the last two weeks.

TUESDAY: You ain't tied to this porch, go home.

THURSDAY: I am just saying I feel like a watchdog.

SATURDAY: That's cause you are.

TUESDAY: She needs to be protected.

THURSDAY: But do you really think Doctor John has the nerve to throw something up on this porch?

TUESDAY: Not as long as we are out here.

SATURDAY: I know that's right.

(Doctor John strolls up the street.)

DOCTOR JOHN: Evening, ladies.

WOMEN OF VIEUX CARRÉ: *(Standing)* Evening.

DOCTOR JOHN: No need for all that—sit down. I wasn't planning to come up those steps.

SATURDAY: What's that in your hand, Doctor John?

DOCTOR JOHN: Just a little something for one of my clients.

77

TUESDAY: It's awful late to be doing business.

DOCTOR JOHN: My work is not dependent on the day.

SATURDAY: No, I guess it is around midnight that you get started.

DOCTOR JOHN: So, the old hag sent you over here to protect the new queen.

TUESDAY: It ain't been decided yet.

DOCTOR JOHN: It was decided a year ago.

SATURDAY: Sanité Dédé will be on the throne St. John's Eve.

DOCTOR JOHN: But Marie Laveau will dance with the redfish.

(*Blackout.*)

ACT II
Scene 4

Setting: The next day, early evening. June 19, 1821. Front room in Laveau cottage.

At Rise: *Colette, wearing a sapphire necklace and gown, is seated. Marie, in black dress and knotted white tignon, stands at the table arranging hair supplies.*

COLETTE: Honestly, I was shocked when I heard you were taking clients.

MARIE: I don't know why—you were the one that said I should be a hairdresser.

COLETTE: But just all of a sudden? I mean, I have barely seen you all year. Every time I come by this house is like a dark tomb waiting to bury you. The light is back in your eyes . . . but you are not quite the same.

MARIE: What do you need done this evening?

COLETTE: The Governor's Ball starts in two hours.

MARIE: You will be the most beautiful woman in the room.

COLETTE: Cut the bullshit, Marie. What brought on this change? Have you got a new man?

(Marie clutches her stomach.)

I knew it! There is only one way to get over a man. Put a new one in your bed. I hope to God he is French and not some dayworker. Who is he? And don't hold out!

MARIE: Why does everything have to be about a man?

COLETTE: Because we are women. What the hell?

(Marie lights a candle at the altar.)

79

MARIE: There is no man, Colette. But you are right—I have changed, because I finally found the strength to bury Jacques.

COLETTE: Good. That son of a bitch didn't deserve a year of your mourning. Walking out on you like that when you lost the baby.

MARIE: Please, let's not talk about it.

COLETTE: Life can be so tough. Honestly, I don't even know if I should go tonight.

MARIE: You've changed too.

COLETTE: My head is about ready to come off. I have the worst headache.

(Marie pulls a few hair strands away from Colette's forehead.)

MARIE: Your forehead is damp. Do you have fever?

COLETTE: I am not sure . . . his wife will be there.

MARIE: Is that what has you troubled?

COLETTE: It is making me nervous.

MARIE: Perhaps you should lie down.

COLETTE: No—I want to see what you can do with this hair. And don't worry, I have the money to pay you.

MARIE: I don't want your money, Colette. You were my first client.

COLETTE: You don't work for free now. If you are not going to take a lover you need every coin you earn to take care of yourself. This is business.

MARIE: *(Holding up hair combs with fake hair attached)* Should we add some weight to the hair?

COLETTE: Use both . . . and blue feathers.

MARIE: You will be stunning. Did the captain give you this necklace?

COLETTE: Yes.

MARIE: It goes with your eyes.

COLETTE: Those were his words when he gave it to me. Take it off!

MARIE: Colette.

COLETTE: Get the damn thing off my neck.

MARIE: Hold on, let me unfasten it.

(Marie hands Colette the necklace.)

COLETTE: You are right, Marie, I have changed. But not in a good way.

MARIE: Sapphires in white gold—that is quite an expensive gift.

COLETTE: *(Scratching scalp)* His wife's fat neck will be covered in diamonds and rubies to match her garish hair.

MARIE: You knew he was married. You told me that last year.

COLETTE: Now I wear the necklace of Captain LaCour's whore—I fit the part.

MARIE: Don't cast stones on your spirit, Colette.

(Marie pulls a strand of Colette's hair from comb.)

COLETTE: The Doctor promised me gold on my finger. All he gave me was a headache.

MARIE: What doctor?

COLETTE: Does it matter? My life is ruined.

(Marie pulls another strand of Colette's hair from comb.)

MARIE: What doctor have you been to, Colette?

COLETTE: The Doctor that promises things, who sees the future. You know how much power he has.

MARIE: Are you saying you went out to Bayou Road?

COLETTE: Don't be mad at me. You have been sitting here like a dead woman for a year. There has been no one to talk to. I had to do something.

(Marie examines the two strands of Colette's hair.)

MARIE: So, you paid Doctor John to do what?

COLETTE: Is that my hair?

MARIE: *(Examining Colette's scalp)* What did that bastard give you?

COLETTE: A charm bag. Is my hair falling out?

MARIE: There is no way you are going to the Governor's Ball tonight. I have to treat your scalp.

(Marie makes a paste from a small jar of soda ash mixed with water.)

COLETTE: Am I losing my hair? Tell me!

MARIE: You have lice.

COLETTE: There's lice in my hair? Are you serious?

MARIE: We need to kill the eggs before they hatch. Take off your gown.

COLETTE: Unfasten it—my skin is crawling.

(Marie unfastens Colette's gown, revealing a lace petticoat, satin corset, and string holding a coarse homemade bag of gris-gris.)

MARIE: What is this around your neck?

COLETTE: *(Removing gris-gris bag)* It's what that son of a bitch gave me.

MARIE: *(Applying soda ash to Colette's hair)* Lice attach to the scalp to breed. Stop freaking out, Colette, we will kill the eggs. We have to apply ash soda to your scalp so I can pick them out of your head.

(Marie picks lice out of Colette's scalp with comb, throws them in bucket.)

COLETTE: If my father was still alive he would kill him.

MARIE: When is the last time you washed your hair?

COLETTE: Four or five weeks.

MARIE: What do you mean, four or five weeks?

COLETTE: Doctor John told me not to strip the natural oils . . . to keep this bag near my breasts and not wash my hair.

MARIE: And you paid him to tell you that? You can go five or six days without washing your hair but not four or five weeks.

COLETTE: I should never have gone out there. His whole yard crawling with cats and goats and possums—filth everywhere. That damn Doctor John gave me lice!

MARIE: I think we've got all the eggs.

(Marie mixes small bottles of oils in bowl.)

COLETTE: What is that?

MARIE: Eucalyptus and tea tree oil. We are going to leave this on your hair for an hour, then wash it with vinegar and peppermint.

COLETTE: I don't want to be alone. Can I stay here with you tonight?

MARIE: Of course. I will repeat the treatment after your hair is clean.

COLETTE: I kept thinking if that witch doctor had the power to drive Jacques from you, he could get rid of the captain's wife. It was such a bitch thing to do. Please forgive me.

MARIE: Hold still.

COLETTE: Wouldn't Captain LaCour's wife just love to know that his whore had lice in her hair?

MARIE: Quit calling yourself a whore.

COLETTE: You don't know the half of it—I am being punished for this plaçage *(touching scalp)*.

MARIE: Don't touch your scalp. I need to wrap it.

COLETTE: Give me the mirror.

(Colette gazes at herself in the mirror as Marie expertly wraps the white cotton cloth.)

Could you imagine if I were to walk in the Governor's Ball like this? I won't be able to sleep tonight.

MARIE: It will be over in a few days.

COLETTE: There is a woman on Commons that shaved her head when her man left her. Is love worth losing your hair?

MARIE: Not if he is a man with a wife, Colette. You should think of your future.

COLETTE: What future do I have?

(Marie places her hand over Colette's as they stare at Colette's reflection in the mirror.)

MARIE: I see laughter from a brown-skinned man with kind eyes. He loves the smell of fresh cut flowers—they remind him of skin he would like to touch. This is a husband that will love his wife long after her hair is gray.

COLETTE: You sure about that?

MARIE: He goes to noon Mass at St. Louis every Sunday. Forget this indiscretion . . . let him find you in prayer.

COLETTE: Really? You expect me to go wait in church for some man to find me? I am sorry, but I don't have that kind of faith in your mirror.

MARIE: It is not the mirror—it is in your reflection.

COLETTE: So, all of a sudden you can just read the future? What do you see between me and Captain LaCour? That is what I am trying to find out.

MARIE: We should stop right now.

COLETTE: You are the one that started this. Please, I need to know.

MARIE: Give me your hand. *(Taking Colette's hand)* Blessed Virgin, guide my sight. I see you waiting in an ivory camisole with four lavender roses on each strap.

COLETTE: That was last Thursday!

MARIE: She is a sight of beauty, Holy Mother. *(Dropping Colette's hand)* Oh. He hurt you.

COLETTE: Yes.

MARIE: *(Grasping Colette's hand)* He is coming into your bedroom smoking a cigar. You don't say a word.

COLETTE: Not a word.

MARIE: He is looking at you—his mustache curls up on the left side. He is dropping something on your camisole—a lit cigar!

COLETTE: Yes. He burned holes in my camisole, then put those sapphires around my neck. How the hell can you see that?

MARIE: It is all right here, under the vein of love on the fourth finger of your left hand. But that is not what caused your trouble. Captain LaCour has a strange fetish for your feet.

COLETTE: Oh my God, Marie, I didn't want to tell you or anyone. That is why I feel like such a whore.

MARIE: When did this start?

COLETTE: I am not sure—maybe four or five weeks ago.

MARIE: Since you started wearing that gris-gris around your neck?

COLETTE: He's been doing unnatural things with my feet . . . filthy. I can't talk about it.

MARIE: *(Opening the gris-gris bag)* Doctor John put a chicken foot around your neck.

COLETTE: Oh my God, is that what's in there? He told me if I opened it, it would kill me.

MARIE: And you believed him—of course you did. Take off your shoes and stockings.

(Colette removes shoes and stockings.)

You came in here spreading that man's evil from the soles of your feet to the hair on your head. I call upon the spirit to cleanse this woman.

(Marie pours holy water around Colette's feet.)

COLETTE: You are scaring me.

MARIE: We must break Captain LaCour's fetish. *(Sprinkles holy water on chicken foot)* I call upon the spirit to twist open and gnarl this foot. *(Cutting the chicken foot into small pieces)* I call upon the spirit to breathe the tendons of this chicken into the eyes of Captain LaCour. *(Dropping pieces of chicken foot into bucket with lice)* Let the sight of Colette's feet cause blood to drip from his eyes . . . all the days of his life.

(Marie throws the contents of the bucket into the fireplace below the altar, then makes the sign of the cross.)

COLETTE: You just burned it off me. What is going on?

MARIE: I need to be alone—and you need some rest.

COLETTE: But how did you see those things?

MARIE: I don't know, but you must never speak a word of this—to anyone.

COLETTE: I won't, I promise.

MARIE: Go in my bedroom and lie down.

COLETTE: My God, you just pulled all the ugly truth out of my guts.

MARIE: The Blessed Virgin holds all our secrets.

(Lights dim.)

Ariel Lucius as **COLETTE DELACROIX**

ACT II
Scene 5

Setting: A few minutes after midnight, June 20, 1821. Bedroom of Laveau cottage.

At Rise: *Thunder erupts. Colette lies sleeping on the bed as Jacques appears soaking wet, searching for Marie, circling the bed.*

JACQUES: I can't get back to you, woman. Your hair is all tangled up inside me . . . keep dreaming you lost the baby, had that dream nine times so it must be right. And I am glad. You hear me—I am glad because no baby of mine is going to be raised by a witch. That is what you are: a goddamn witch . . . that ripped out my heart. That's why I shipped out. Been up to Boston, over to Cuba on a Baltimore clipper. Wherever we unload the cargo, I just keep going. Sometimes I look up at the sails when the wind hits them and see that first time—how you looked lying naked across those white wedding sheets.

(Jacques rips sheets from bed. Colette in a dream state, sits up gazing at her reflection in Marie's hand mirror.)

COLETTE: The blue feathers go with my eyes.

JACQUES: *(Unwrapping Colette's tignon)* How many months have I stood, staring out at the waves hitting the side of the ship, unwrapping your tignon in my mind's eye.

COLETTE: You have rough hands for a hairdresser.

JACQUES: *(Running his hands through Colette's hair)* What you doing with all these snakes crawling through your scalp?

COLETTE: Are you the Doctor?

JACQUES: No, it's me, Marie's husband.

COLETTE: You've spoiled her supper table for a whole year. You got no business coming around here.

JACQUES: I got something to say to Marie.

(Sanité Dédé and Women of Vieux Carré enter.)

SANITÉ DÉDÉ: Your Catholic wife is dead, Jacques Paris.

COLETTE: Don't believe her. She is not dead!

(Women of Vieux Carré make the sign of the cross in reverent motion.)

WOMEN OF VIEUX CARRÉ:
The tears of the mother of Marie.
The tears of the mother of Marie.
The tears of the mother of Marie.

COLETTE: This is not Marie's funeral.

SANITÉ DÉDÉ: You don't belong here, Colette Delacroix.

COLETTE: I am reading Marie's future.

SANITÉ DÉDÉ: Give me that mirror.

COLETTE: Go away. *(Staring into the hand mirror)* She is coming out of
the water on Lake Pontchartrain with seven candles on her head. Now
she is dancing across the lake. You are standing on the shore with a
bucket of fish to feed the multitude. You are waiting . . . waiting for
Marie Laveau.

*(African drumming comes up as Sanité Dédé's eyes fall back into her head.
Women of Vieux Carré gyrate mounted by spirit. Colette stares into the
hand mirror viewing a future event.)*

SANITÉ DÉDÉ:
Calinda Calinda Bomba hen Bomba hen
Eh, ye, ye Mamzelle Marie
Ya, ye ye, li konin tou, gris-gris

WOMEN OF VIEUX CARRÉ:
> *Ay yea, yea Mamzelle Marie, Ya, yea, yea, she knows all the gris-gris*
> *She had gone to school with the old crocodiles*
> *Oh, yes, yea, Mamzelle Marie*
> *She knows well the Grand Zombi!*

(Marie appears soaking wet in a white camisole with a crown of lit candles on her head.)

MARIE: Danbala! Shango! Ogun! From the islands of the Caribbean to the West Coast of Africa, let me smell my sacrifice on this ground.

JACQUES: Marie?

MARIE: I buried you, Jacques Paris.

JACQUES: I never stopped loving you.

MARIE: I know.

JACQUES: They drove me out.

MARIE: No. You took yourself away from me. Now go and be blessed.

(Jacques wanders out of the room. Marie stares out as African drums come up calling Marie to remembrance.)

WOMEN OF VIEUX CARRÉ: What do you see, Marie?

MARIE: I see seven African women with full sets of teeth in a slave pen on Commons. Saloppe, Eliza, Comtesse, Domingo, Ginger, Angele, Levasseur. They are all of childbearing years. Shipped from the Port of Havana, Cuba.

SANITÉ DÉDÉ: What do you see, Marie?

MARIE: I see nine African warriors on the auction block branded with the fleur-de-lis. Yoruba, Ibo, Hausa, Fon, Ewe, Ashanti, Akan, Congalese, Senagalese. *(Pulling a redfish from her breast)* Come into me my sons and daughters. I am one with the First Ancestor. On this hallowed spot in this sacred city, we gather the nations to remember!

(African drums beat with frenzy. Bras-Coupé appears. Marie dances with redfish in traditional African celebratory movement. Women of Vieux Carré and Sanité Dédé join the powerful dance, which ends as Bras-Coupé leads Marie out.)

COLETTE: Wait for me!

SANITÉ DÉDÉ: *(Taking hand mirror from Colette)* Erase the future that Marie carries. You should not remember this night.

(Sanité Dédé and Women of Vieux Carré leave as drums are silenced.)

COLETTE: *(Still in a dream state)* Come back. I can't see where you are going, Marie. Don't put her in a casket with that chicken foot. *(Feeling scalp)* Is my hair falling out? *(Picking up head wrap and tying it sloppily on head)* Am I in a dream, some strange dream? God, I can't remember what it was. Damn it. Marie is changing. I am changing. You never know when the lady inside is going to hold up the mirror and say, "Walk into tomorrow."

(Lights crossfade to outside porch.)

ACT II
Scene 6

Setting: The next evening, June 21, 1821. Front steps of Laveau cottage.

At Rise: *Women of Vieux Carré, with lighted candles, are holding watch over the cottage. A troubled Mary Earle walks up the street with her laundry cart.*

MARY EARLE: I am looking for John Earle.

SATURDAY: He ain't been up on St. Ann.

TUESDAY: Why don't you go see Sanité Dédé? Maybe she could help you out.

MARY EARLE: I don't need a nurse—I need my man to come home.

THURSDAY: Sorry for your trouble, Mary Earle.

MARY EARLE: *(Pulling a knife from her pocket)* Oh, I am gonna take care of it. He is coming home.

(Mary Earle drags her cart down the street.)

TUESDAY: Mary Earle been out to see Doctor John.

THURSDAY: Cut the hair from her privates, laid them in John Earle's old boot.

SATURDAY: Put three coins in a water glass by the bed stand.

TUESDAY: Wrapped up the bed sheet from the last time they was together.

THURSDAY: Gave Doctor John half of her rent money.

SATURDAY: John Earle is over on Esplanade, laying between Sophina Jefferson's big legs.

TUESDAY: She about to do something to that bitch.

93

THURSDAY: John Earle better bring his ass home.

(Doctor John strolls up the street.)

DOCTOR JOHN: Evening, ladies.

(Women of Vieux Carré stand.)

Now there is no need for that, I wasn't trying to come up those steps.

TUESDAY: You ain't got no clients on St. Ann Street, Jean Montanée.

DOCTOR JOHN: Girl, you don't know what I got.

(Marie opens door and comes out on porch.)

The young mulatress, Mamzelle Marie.

MARIE: You women go on home.

SATURDAY: Sanité Dédé said for us stay out here until midnight.

MARIE: I've got this.

(Women of Vieux Carré leave the porch. Marie and Doctor John face off.)

DOCTOR JOHN: Been waiting a year for you to come out on that porch.

MARIE: Stay away from Colette Delacroix.

(Marie throws Doctor John's bag of gris-gris at his feet.)

DOCTOR JOHN: *(Picks up bag, puts it around his neck, and conceals it inside his shirt)* I put my special blend in this bag for Colette. When they are sick from love and their bellies are aching to be filled, they come for snakes, powders, dirt, whatever I give them. But I appreciate your concern. It has been a year since he left, Widow Paris.

MARIE: Yes, Jacques is gone.

DOCTOR JOHN: You could bring him back.

MARIE: There will never be a man in my bed that comes in the shadows.

DOCTOR JOHN: You looking at one in the flesh right here.

MARIE: I hate you.

DOCTOR JOHN: Hate me? We are both at the crossroads, little sister.

MARIE: You know nothing about me.

DOCTOR JOHN: I'm closer to you than your own life vein.

MARIE: You bring nothing but trouble.

DOCTOR JOHN: I have come for the queen, about to be born. And the people will chant: Marie, Marie Laveau.

MARIE: *(Turning to go inside)* I can't be here.

DOCTOR JOHN: Sanité Dédé was here before you.

MARIE: What?

DOCTOR JOHN: Yeah, we get to that now. I was the first to have her.

MARIE: I don't believe you.

DOCTOR JOHN: *(Coming up the steps)* Ask her who came into her belly in the sugarcane. Sanité Dédé walked with the serpent through me!

MARIE: You are a liar!

DOCTOR JOHN: Sanité Dédé's time has passed. You will be on the throne. *(Feeling faint, he rubs the back of his neck.)* There is a lot I could teach you if you let me in your bed.

MARIE: You dirty old man—I honor the spirit.

DOCTOR JOHN: *(Rubbing his forehead)* I see you taking clients—using the power.

MARIE: Not like you. Putting false dreams in desperate women.

DOCTOR JOHN: Giving hope so they can get out of bed. *(Coughing)* Let me come inside.

MARIE: You will never pass through my door!

DOCTOR JOHN: *(Almost losing his balance, then derogatorily)* Jesus Christ. There is something lurking out here.

MARIE: I won't use it for evil, like you.

DOCTOR JOHN: *(Agitated)* You don't know what you gonna do when the power comes on you and the snake is in your belly. Once you stand at the crossroads, that's it. Telling me what you gonna do and what you not gonna do. *(Feeling nauseous, he sits down on the steps.)* I ain't got time to hear all that. I . . . I ain't got time . . .

MARIE: *(Standing over him)* You are a rotten seed that ate from the Tree of Life. It doesn't belong to you, Jean Montanée.

DOCTOR JOHN: *(Summoning up strength, he attempts to stand)* When you see me coming down the street, you'll know what I am walking with. *(Bending over in real pain.)*

MARIE: *(Without concern for him)* I see you right here. Your big head with one eye attached to twenty tentacles slithering down the alley. They are going to call you Bayou John—the dirtbag that comes in the shadows.

DOCTOR JOHN: Are you trying to fix me? *(Dry heaving.)*

MARIE: Healing and killing are both at the crossroads.

DOCTOR JOHN: Be careful—I can bleed you, body and soul. *(Coughing.)*

MARIE: Use that evil eye behind your forehead to watch me honor the spirit.

DOCTOR JOHN: *(Ripping the gris-gris bag off his neck)* What did you put in this bag, bitch?

MARIE: Marie Laveau. Now get off my porch.

(Marie raises her hands majestically and hits the air, causing Doctor John to be thrown from the steps. Doctor John falls to the ground then stumbles down the street dry heaving and coughing.)

ACT II
Scene 7

Setting: Afternoon of St. John's Eve, June 23, 1821. Front room of Laveau cottage.

At Rise: *Marie stands at the table preparing roots as Mary Earle, struggling up the steps with severe pain in her leg, enters with laundry basket.*

MARIE: Put the basket down, Mary Earle.

MARY EARLE: Guess you heard me and John Earle had some trouble.

MARIE: He's not going far.

MARY EARLE: Month behind on my rent. Give him all my week's money to get some meat. Come to find out he go around all my customers asking for an advance on clothes not spoiled.

MARIE: That leg needs your attention.

MARY EARLE: I don't think the Doctor set it right.

MARIE: What doctor you been to?

MARY EARLE: The one on Bayou Road . . .

MARIE: Pull up your skirt.

MARY EARLE: I got three more loads to pick up on Rampart.

MARIE: John Earle cut you with a knife.

MARY EARLE: He ashamed because he married a cripple.

MARIE: You should be ashamed you let him back in your house.

MARY EARLE: When he's not drinking, he's a good man. Sophina Jefferson the one poured all that whiskey down his throat.

MARIE: She has been sick with chills and sweats since last week.

MARY EARLE: What is that to me?

MARIE: Sophina Jefferson is not the only woman in New Orleans with big legs.

MARY EARLE: What you trying to say?

MARIE: Sit down. Show me what he did to you.

MARY EARLE: I been looking after the puss—it don't have a smell.

(She lifts up her skirt and Marie examines the blood flow above the gaping wound.)

Oh God, no please . . . don't touch it.

MARIE: Look at me. This is gangrene. Do you understand?

MARY EARLE: It wasn't his fault. It was an accident.

MARIE: Stop lying. Do you want to lose this leg?

MARY EARLE: No. Lord, help me, Widow.

(Marie pours rum on the open wound at the knee. Mary Earle holds back an agonizing scream.)

MARIE: *(Packing the wound)* You have to be off this leg a month.

MARY EARLE: How am I gonna make rent? I am already a month behind.

MARIE: John Earle has two hands.

MARY EARLE: You know how hard it is for our men to get work. He been up and down the levees trying—nobody want to hire him.

MARIE: How much is your rent?

MARY EARLE: Fourteen dollars.

MARIE: Here is two months.

MARY EARLE: God knows you is a saint. People taking notice.

MARIE: John Earle must not know of our business here.

MARY EARLE: He gonna ask how I made two month's rent when he comes back.

MARIE: Make up a lie.

MARY EARLE: I paid the rest of my rent money to put something on Sophina. That's why he cut me.

MARIE: John Earle is fighting his demons on your legs.

MARY EARLE: It was that woman that messed up his mind. Wish she was dead.

MARIE: Get up.

MARY EARLE: I got needs, Marie. You still a young, beautiful woman. You understand.

MARIE: Walk out of here.

MARY EARLE: Don't be angry when I'm carrying so much trouble.

MARIE: I won't speak of the trouble inside me, but when life brings a sorrow song, carry it with dignity. The lust in John Earle is your enemy, not Sophina Jefferson.

MARY EARLE: I don't see that—but I ain't walking with the power like you.

MARIE: You have your own power, Mary Earle. You are just sleeping on it. All the conjure in New Orleans can't stop John Earle from cutting up your legs. You got to be the one to end it.

MARY EARLE: I ain't that strong.

MARIE: You have to try.

MARY EARLE: But he is still my husband . . .

(Mary Earle picks up basket and walks out of the house.)

MARIE: Pray to St. Anthony.

(Marie lights a candle at the altar and makes the sign of the cross. Sanité Dédé appears at the door in a white dress, white tignon, basket, and bucket. Marie kisses her on the cheek, inviting her in.)

SANITÉ DÉDÉ: *(Taking white dress out of basket)* Put this on. Brought a bucket of redfish to fry up out at Bayou St. John. Fire has already started—they been cooking gumbo out there all afternoon.

MARIE: I don't know if I am ready.

SANITÉ DÉDÉ: Oh, you are ready—Doctor John lost his voice. Had the nerve to come and see me to clear out his throat.

MARIE: Guinea peppers will do that if you are not careful.

SANITÉ DÉDÉ: The spirit is guiding your hands.

(Sanité Dédé crosses to altar.)

MARIE: There is nothing on my altar.

(Sanité Dédé locates a bundle in black cloth and unwraps it, revealing a statue of Virgin Mary.)

SANITÉ DÉDÉ: Lie to yourself, not Sanité Dédé. You been praying to your Virgin to bring Paris back, but since that didn't work you wrapped her up—turned her upside down and offered your prayer to Ayida-Weddo.

MARIE: I found a lock of his hair under the bed. Can you believe that—after a whole year?

SANITÉ DÉDÉ: The spirit is testing you, Marie.

MARIE: I wasn't praying for him to come back—only to be safe, wherever he is.

SANITÉ DÉDÉ: You are a queen, not the wife he walked out on.

MARIE: The Ancestor never leaves me . . . even when I take communion.

SANITÉ DÉDÉ: It is the same for all our people.

MARIE: I can't heal others if I can't heal myself.

SANITÉ DÉDÉ: There is another man coming, when you are ready he will find you. But *this* is your life's work.

MARIE: I have seen him—and my children. But I will never marry again.

SANITÉ DÉDÉ: No, you will be Widow Paris your whole life.

MARIE: To remind me who I was the night I bled.

SANITÉ DÉDÉ: You had to die and resurrect to walk with the Ancestors. Your first head-washing will be tonight on St. John's Eve. Through us the gate opens.

(The sound of African drums fills the room.)

MARIE: They are coming to dance on my head, turn sweat into wine, until time carries me back, to kiss the flesh of a lesser lover.

SANITÉ DÉDÉ: Our people need this power.

MARIE: The drums are raging. Blue water comes rushing in an ancient memory. It is going to take me places tonight . . . places in the spirit. No flesh will ever be as sweet.

SANITÉ DÉDÉ: It is time to go.

MARIE: Even when old bones cover me. The people will remember.

(African drums continue to pound as they leave. Blackout.)

END OF PLAY

ACKNOWLEDGMENTS

A special thanks to the Dillard Theatre Arts Program, the first and longest-running theatre degree-granting HBCU Black Theatre Arts program in the United States under the guidance of Professor Cortheal Clark, who believed in this script even before the first draft was completed. Clark's authentic design of a Creole cottage for the Dillard production transported the audience to St. Ann Street in New Orleans circa 1820. I would also like to thank David I. L. Poole, who spent countless late nights providing dramaturgical feedback on every line in the play and brought this piece to its feet through his visionary direction. I owe much to my mentor, Igbo Chief Dr. Ernest Emenyonu, for opening the gate to African traditional rituals and ceremonies. Finally, my heartfelt gratitude to Dean Bruce Duell, Zen Zadih Pace, Desiree Reine Duell, David Michael Henderson, and Diana Lynn Morgan for inspiring my work through their own creative risks.

ABOUT THE AUTHOR

Carolyn Nur Wistrand is an award-winning playwright and educator. Her plays have been staged in New York City, Los Angeles, Chicago, Dallas, Houston, Savannah, Atlanta, Flint, Omaha, Detroit, and New Orleans. A recipient of the MACC/NEA Award, a NEH Summer Fellowship, and winner of the Mario-Fratti-Fred Newman International Playwriting Competition, she is a professor of English and Drama at Dillard University in New Orleans.

9 781959 569183